The
Mistress of Desire
&
The Orchid Lover
Book II
The Quest
One Love In A Lifetime

A novel by

J. A. Jackson

Acknowledgments

To my readers and fans I am forever grateful. Thank you.

A special thanks to my sisters Kay, Shelia and Marie. And my brothers Ray and Eric I thank you all for your wonderful support. Next thank you Mark "Doc" for all that you do. I appreciate all your help and support.

Next, a special thanks to my friends, J. Marie Owens, Marian Askew, Anna Griffin, Bernice Willis, Zina Slaughter, Stephanie Griffin, Sondra Jennings, Lan Vo, Linda Nguyen, Keith Rovin, Lisa Earnest and Lisa Riley.

Next, a special thanks to my BFF's who's love is always with me...
Joycelyn Lewis, Mary Shields, Lenise Gibson and Petra Ramirez. I will love you ladies always. Thanks for being a part of my life.

For Rossi, Randy, Daddy & Mommy my love always....

Prologue

The room was silent except for the echoing sound of Nona's vintage alligator peep-toed pumps as they slammed across the floor, as she charged in.

"You are late!"

"Now Glenda," Nona excitedly exhaled. "You know I told you I had to go to Pointe Richmond, today? My favorite store was having their fifty percent off annual sale."

Surprise and embarrassment ran a swift race across Glenda's face. "Did you go to Ancient Ways? Oh, I'd forgotten."

Nona hurried over and thrust a bag in Glenda's hand. "See, I got you something."

"Thank you," Glenda muttered, with an apologetic tone in her voice.

Nona turned and made a beeline across the room. "Oh, and here's yours Consuelo," she said excitedly, handing her a bag.

Nona sighed heavily. "For some reason, the traffic on Highway 80 was ridiculous today."

"Thank you, Nona," Consuelo smiled and let her eyes settle on Nona's for a second before she nodded agreement. "It's true, about the traffic being heavy on Highway 80, today. Just this morning I saw it on the news, something to do with a big rig turning over," she said, with a heavy Spanish accent.

Nona leaned in close and whispered. "Thanks for having my back Consuelo. By the way, I picked you up some that Herb man's best sage, the one you like."

"Excellent," Consuelo replied with a look of surprise. "You must have read my mind. I was almost out."

Glenda cleared her throat. "Ladies, now that we're all here now. Let's begin."

Nona put her hand boldly on her hip. "Begin what? Consuelo and I have no idea why you summoned us here, with Halloween just around the corner we all have things to do. Why are we here?"

"Didn't I tell you? We are here because of Delmar Devereaux."

"You called us here because of that asshole?" Nona inquired. "You have got to be kidding me. Everyone knows, Delmar carries a truckload of bullshit wherever he goes."

Consuelo fixed Glenda with a stern look and interrupted her, pounding her with questions in rapid Spanish. "And you want us to help him? What has he done? Mother Mary, I pray, please tell me he hasn't killed someone?"

Nona turned to Consuelo and Glenda. "If he did, I say let him rot in jail. He deserves too."

"I righteously agree!" Consuelo added, rolling her "r's."

Glenda stood and glance back at Nona and Consuelo and sighed, "Aye, yai yai yai yai!" She shook her head. "Ladies you have no compassion for a fallen man. Didn't you hear me. I said, Delmar Devereaux, has come to us for help."

"Help?" Nona and Consuelo said in Unisom.

"Yes, Ladies, he has."

"Well, where is he?" Consuelo asked.

"He had to leave early, but no worries. I have captured a memory of his visit with me today. We can all talk to Delmar in just a few seconds," she said, walking over to the huge cauldron pot sitting on an open fire. The pot bubbled as steamed escaped and evaporated into the air.

Glenda D'Goodwrench, reached into her pocket and pulled out a small clear glass vial, that contained a bluish liquid.

"Ladies, please come closer," she said softly, as she slowly opened the vial and gently poured the contents into the cauldron.

A heavy primeval smell filled the air as the bluish liquid ascended into the air and circled until a frisson… Then slowly the face of Delmar Devereaux, appeared.

"Check him out," Nona stated.

After a moment of hesitation, Delmar spoke. "I am so sorry I had to leave early, ladies. I meant no disrespect."

"None taken, right ladies?" Glenda asked.

Consuelo and Nona nodded their heads and muttered agreement.

Delmar's voice was sad and serious. "I come to ask the three of you for your help. I have nowhere else to turn. The courts won't help me. The legal system is useless," his words tumbled out. "You see, for it was I, who started my problem in the first place, and well the courts won't even hear my case," he sighed heavily.

Glenda sighed. "This sounds serious if you can't use your money to persuade the courts."

"It is serious," Delmar assured them. "Let me go back to the beginning. Perhaps you were aware of my case in court almost a year ago, concerning the twin sons, that Tiara Blake, had?"

"Yes, of course, it was all over the news," Consuelo stated, in an excited Spanish accent.

"Yeah, I heard all about it too," Nona said glumly. "The DNA found you were not the father and those test are normally 100% accurate."

"Yes, they are supposed to be. But there are ways around them," Delmar paused. "You see a rootworker, a spell caster. She assured me, that she could cast a spell that would exclude me as the father of the twins."

Glenda interrupted. "Yes, but everyone knows that DNA is 100 percent foolproof and it doesn't lie. No spellcaster or rootworker can mess with biological DNA."

"Glenda is right," Nona stated. "DNA tests are considered infallible – they are the gold standard in court."

"In a manner of speaking, you are both correct," Delmar replied. "Like I said earlier, there are ways around things. There are "those" who know things. And when I went looking for help. I went to the best."

"If you used the best, then why are you here?" Consuelo asked.

Delmar hovering image gave her enigmatic smile. He took a deep breath and his voice softened. "What I failed to realize is … He hesitated and looked up. "Do you believe in past lives?"

Glenda looked back at Nona and Consuelo. The three of them smiled.

"Of course we do," Glenda answered for the three of them.

Nona spoke up. "It is a known fact, among us, we believe, in each life, we are here seeking the companions of our past, who come into this life to play, an important role in the life that we live, now."

"This cycle can go on many lifetimes," Consuelo added, with a heavy Spanish accent.

"I agree with the three of you," Delmar replied. "I've recently learned of my connection to a young woman, in a past life," he said caressing the line of his jaw. "I... I Didn't realize how important it was for us to meet in this life. And now that I know…"

"Oh, my goodness!" Nona interrupted him. "Let me guess, she is the mother of the twins. The sons, you denied being the father of in a court of law."

"And the DNA test has excluded you and now you want to turn back the clock," Consuelo stated, in a prevalent Spanish accent.

"Ladies," Glenda said. "Let Delmar finish telling us his story."

"But we have the story," Nona said.

"No," Glenda interrupted. "We do not have the full story. Do we Delmar?"

"Bad things happened," Consuelo said, in a heavy Spanish accent. "I can feel it."

Delmar took a deep breath. "You see, I traveled to see the best performer of magic in the state of California, she lives in the enchanted forest in Elfin.

Nona shook her head in disbelief. "Oh, my God! You mean, Elfin Forest, in Escondido? Why she's the most powerful white witch of them all!"

"You went to see Mary?" Consuelo gasped.

"You consulted with the White Witch of Elfin Forest?" Glenda D'Goodwrench yelled. "And you have the gall to ask the help of a descendant of Marie Laveau, and the great family of the Oshun of Santería Cuba?"

"You left out your great family heritage, Glenda. The D'Goodwrench family has long been practicing white magic in this great state of California," Nona added.

Delmar's eyes widen. "So, are you ladies telling me you cannot handle a minor spell cast by an old dead legend from California's mining days?" He asked rolling his eyes, looking disgusted. "And, here I thought I was seeking the help of the best and the brightest and you three are nothing but a bunch of losers…"

"Shut-up Delmar!" Glenda's bellowing voice interrupted him, as her eyes filled with rage. "We will not be insulted by the likes of you!" She spat twice, and her cat Pinky appeared out of nowhere and jumped into her arms, as Consuelo and Nona moved in closer to her. A thick blanket of fog rolled out of nowhere and surround them.

Then they vanished into thin air.

"Ladies… Ladies! I apologize!" Delmar yelled as the vapor that was his frame slowly dissipated.

Chapter 1

Possibilities Life has to offer...

Camille fought back the desire to walk over to Tiara and slap some sense into her. She hated it when Tiara acted slutty in public. It made her want to go postal on her, thank God she couldn't because she was sitting there holding one of Tiara' twins and she didn't want to startle the baby.

"Tiara Blake! How can you be so obtuse!" Eris Simeon barked in a jailhouse voice. "Why can't you keep your hands to yourself? We're in a hospital for Christ sake!"

Tiara frowned and closed the gap between them. Looking innocent she said. "What? He gave me a love tap first, besides I know him. He's just a friend."

"Camille Baptiste-Garcia, talk to your friend," Eris commanded.

Camille slowly shook her head and looked up. "I guess you are feeling well like the doctor said, huh Tiara?"

Tiara's lips erupted in a big smile "Yes, I am, and you heard the doctor give me a clean bill of health and my vaginoplasty worked like magic.That means I can start screwing again, and I got just the man in mind to do the job."

"Come on, you're not thinking of sleeping with that orderly?" Eris asked. "What if he's married?"

Tiara shrugged, she didn't have the heart to tell Eris the man she really wanted to have sex with was Delmar Devereaux . After the nine months of carrying the twins and almost a year of fighting their biological father in court. She still wanted him. Still let Eris think what she wanteds she thought and said. "Just so you know Eris, he's a anesthesiologist, and not an orderly. Besides, I didn't see no wedding ring on his middle finger and anyway, he groped me first, or didn't you see that?"

"Camille, talk to your friend," Eris said, shifting the little boy from one hip to the other. "And here I am holding your son while you're making plans to have a screw feast with an orderly."

"Yes, I intend to do some serious fucking, now that my

vagina has healed from the stitches those two-little big-headed boys gave me. Momma's horny now."

Eris rolled her eyes. "Tiara! Don't say horny around the babies, please!"

"Those two two-little big-headed boys ought to know by now that their momma ain't the Virgin Mary. Mommy got needs, and she needs to start finding those two a father," Tiara said, glancing in Eris' direction.

She watched as Eris played with her son. "Eris, I wouldn't need to go out gallivanting about looking for a baby daddy if you would help me"

Eris laughed. "Hell no, Tiara. I ain't giving my matchmaking business a bad name trying to help a *don't know how to be loyal heifer like you find a man."*

Camille laughed and shook her head as she kept bouncing the little boy sitting in her lap. She knew when to stay out of Tiara and Eris' conversation. Beside it was a joy holding the little fellow in her lap. Jayden and Jaylen were twins and she finally learned how to tell them apart. She was holding Jaylen, he was the serious one. He loved to observe the world around him, like he was taking it all in. Eris was holding his brother Jayden. He was the one with the personality. Laughing and playfully all the time.

Eris began cooing to the baby she held. "You poor, poor baby."

The baby rewarded her making babbling gurgling sounds and smiling back at her.

"Thank God little Jaylen wasn't traumatized by his mother's scandalous behavior," Eris said.

Eris turned her attention to the baby in her arms. It hurt her heart to think that Tiara was this child's mother.

A frown touched her brow, thinking these two beautiful twin boys would have to be brought up by such a mother as Tiara. She wished they were hers. She didn't have long with her fantasy wish when she noticed out of the corner of her eye the tall guy Tiara had been flirting with earlier come walking back in to view.

He stood just inside the door, his excellent shape and over six feet tall frame, caused a shadow to fade across the room.

"Look, who's back?" Eris announced.

"Why if it isn't the dangerous looking handsome devil you were flirting with earlier, Tiara. Looks like he's changed into his civilian clothes," Camille replied. "I didn't notice how well he fill out his jeans before," she exhaled. "Dog gone it! There ought to be a law against a man filling out a pair of jeans like that."

Eris and Camille exchanged glances.

"Hey Zack," Tiara said.

"Hey Tiara," he nodded and turned and looked at Camille and Eris. "Ladies it good to see you again."

Camille and Eris nodded in Unisom and said. "Hi Zack."

"What do you want Zack?" Tiara asked.

Zack plastered on a smile and laid on the charm. "Hello again, beautiful. I hope I'm not bothering you, but I forgot to ask if you would like to have lunch with me?"

"When?" Tiara gushed.

"Well, today, or tomorrow, whenever you have the time," Zack replied.

"Oh, yes I would. In fact, today sounds really good," Tiara sighed, turning to look at her best friends.

Tiara's eyes looked pleadingly back at Eris. Her stomach was bundled in knots. She hadn't been out alone with a man since the twins had been born. "Eris, my best friend in the world," she stated lacing her voice and kindness. "Would you mind watching Jaylen, while I go to lunch with Zack, today?"

Eris spun around in her seat. Her hands securely holding little Jaylen. "Tiara," Eris said, sternly, "Have you forgotten you have two sons, twins?"

Tiara smiled big and bright. "Duh! No," she replied. "But I know if you say yes, Camille will agree to keep Jayden. Camille loves me like that. Besides, she knows I haven't been anyplace alone, since the twins were born."

Eris threw her free hand in the air and looked at Tiara like she was a piece of work. "Oh, fine, whatever Tiara, just don't come back from lunch pregnant."

Yeah, I love you too Eris," Tiara replied, taking Zack by the hand. "Come on Zack let's get out of here before they change their minds."

Eris back stiffened. "Hold on Tiara! We haven't been

properly introduced to your friend. What's this guy Zack's full name?"

Tiara froze in her tracks. "Oh, yeah, pardon me. Zackary Vaughn, these two ladies are my oldest and dearest friends. Meet, Eris and Camille," she giggled. "Eris and Camille meet Zack."

"Nice to meet you Zack," Eris and Camille song in Unisom, just as Tiara grabbed Zack by the hand and whisk him out of sight.

Chapter 2
Regrets, Reunions, & Sins of the past

"Eating alone is a bitch!" Delmar Devereaux thought as he walked toward the familiar restaurant.

The Bistro Café, in downtown San Jose, just off First Street and Park Avenue, was normally his favorite place to eat. He thought back on the numerous women he'd brought there over the years. Back in the day, his bringing them here was normally a prelude to one of his sexual exploits.

Making his way into the restaurant he smiled with his thoughts, remembering how his sexual exploits used to be all he ever cared about. He took and discarded more women than he'd care to remember. Now a day's sex, love and everything he ever thought was important had changed for him. Nowadays, his thoughts were forever turning to the twin sons he had discarded like yesterday's newspaper. His definition of what was important had truly shifted.

"Mr. Devereaux, would you like a table by the window?"

Delmar stiffened in surprise when he realized the hostess was speaking to him. He cleared his throat. "No, thank you. I prefer a booth, in the back, private. I'm eating alone," he said, feeling the need to explain.

"No, problem," his hostess said, politely. "Right this way, Mr. Devereaux."

Delmar slid his hands into the pockets of the tailored suit he wore as he followed his hostess.

A few minutes later. "This is perfect," he said, sliding into the private booth.

He leaned back and studied his menu. He'd just started concentrating on what he wanted to eat. When he heard, laughter coming from the booth behind him.

A woman laughed, teasingly. "Are you going to try and eat it all?"

Delmar leaned back attentive and gave the woman's voice some serious thought.

"Yes," a man's voice garbled out, through a mouth full of

food. "I'm just trying to help you keep that gorgeous figure."

The woman let out a sexy hoarse laughed. "Oh, aren't you the considerate one. Thanks, honey!"

Delmar stiffened in surprise. He was sure the woman's voice was familiar. Abruptly, he rose from his booth and walked over to the booth behind him and frowned.

Tiara Blake's mouth fell open.There he stood. The devil himself complete with razor thin moustache. "Delmar! What are you doing here?"

"Madame! What is the mother of my sons doing out? Alone, without them?"Delmar asked but didn't wait for a response. "Whom did you leave my sons with?"

Delmar turned and fixed his gaze on her date. "And who the hell is this!"

Tiara remained silent a moment longer and then licked her lips and let out a dry husky laugh low in her throat. She wasn't about to play into Delmar's game of fifty questions. She took a deep breath and stated. "Looks like today's a day for me to make introductions," she waved her hand dismissively. "Oh, well, if it must be, here goes. Zackary Vaughn, meet my babies' biological daddy, Delmar Devereaux. Unless of course, you ask the courts and they will tell you he paid them a pretty penny to make the evidence state otherwise."

"Hello, Delmar. Or should I say, Mr. Devereaux," Zack snorted in derision? "Sounds like you got skills, getting out of paying child support, I mean."

"Nice to meet you, Zackary. But if you don't mind that's a touchy subject with me, I'd rather not talk about with you," Delmar said, defensively.

Tiara started laughing. "Yeah, that it is. What are you doing here Delmar?"

"Well, I was here having a late lunch alone," Delmar hesitated, his jaw trembled. "But now that I see you. I believe that *"fate"* has intervened and given me a chance to ask to speak with you, privately."

Tiara leaned back in her seat studying him. Her thoughts raced. *Be with me lord, after the mess this joker put me through in that courtroom, she didn't ever want to be alone with him.* She stiffened shaking out of her thoughts and felt the beginning of a headache as her anger poured out in a flash. "You were wrong for the way you treated me in that courtroom Delmar!" Her lip trembled. "You had your lawyers treat me like I was dirt."

Zack watched the exchange been between the two with wide eyed interest. This drama was better than anything he'd find on TV.

"I want to apologize for all of that," Delmar's voice pleaded, as he leaned forward. "In fact, I sincerely regret what I did, and I hope to have a reunion, with you and my sons, very soon. I truly want to be forgiven for my past deeds, for my sins, by you, by my sons, by God."

Tiara looked back at Delmar confused. She shook her head thinking about all the hurt Delmar had brought into her life. She felt a solitary tear gradually roll down her cheek.

Delmar waved his hand. "You see Tiara, I've been reading the bible and I've been speaking to Father Perez..."

Tiara interrupted. "Hold up. You've been speaking with Father Perez? The one from the Church of the Good Shepherd?" She asked, wiping the tear from her cheek. She didn't wait for a response. "Delmar, are you feeling alright? I mean you are not sick or anything?"

"No, I'm not sick. I've just come to my senses. I realize all of the pain I have caused to others," he hung his head. "I am so ashamed at what I've done to my family, my sons, their mother and well, I want to put things right and get back into God's good graces. I want to make amends."

Tiara felt tears filling her eyes. Hearing the sadness in Delmar's voice let her know he really regretted his actions. This was all too confusing. How could she forgive Delmar for all the hurt and pain he caused her? She shook her head feeling conflicted and covered her mouth feeling she was going to let out a sob.

Zack cleared his throat. "I think that's my cue to leave."

Hearing Zack's voice woke her out of her trance. She was sure Delmar was just scheming. He had to be up to something. That was it, she thought, he was just trying to get her sympathy so that he could do something else treacherous to her. It was never good to get caught up in Delmar's drama fest. She was sure he was after something.

Loudly she cleared her throat. "No! Zack! Don't leave!" Tiara yelled, finding her voice. "What you are witnessing here today is a great actor and a bad liar. But then most narcissistic people are," she began clapping her hands. "Bravo Delmar, you almost had me."

She turned her head. "Zack darling, I think it is time we both left and let Mr. Devereaux, finish his lunch, alone. In fact, I think Mr. Devereaux, should pay for our lunch, as well."

Tiara shifted her eyes to Delmar. Their gazes locked. Her eyes glittered with anger. "I will say you are hanging with a better class of people for once Delmar, Father Perez, of the Church of the Good Shepherd, now I would have never thought the devil inside of you would let you get so close to a member of the clergy. But, stranger things have happened in this world," she softly laughed. "Good luck with that. Oh, and the next time you see him tell Father to pray for me, cause I'm going home with Zack here, and I'm going to do my best to fuck his brains out."

Zack whistled loudly. "Damn, I'm one lucky man!"

Tiara rose and grabbed Zack's hand. She would make Zack aware very shortly that she had no intentions of fulfilling what she'd just said. She said all of that for Delmar's benefit only and since she'd made Delmar pay for their meal. She certainly wasn't about to be Zack's dessert.

"Come, Zack, oh and thanks again for lunch Delmar," she said making it a point to cuddle in close to Zack as they made their exit.

Delmar watched her leave and then closed his eyes praying for strength. He'd known getting Tiara to believe that he was telling the truth wouldn't be easy. But God knew what was in his heart and he wasn't going to give up.

Chapter 3

Camille & Desmond Garcia

Camille stretched her nude body and then sat up on the edge of the bed and looked out of the French doors and spotted two geese flying low before landing in the man-made pond, Desmond, had built for her when they'd gotten married.

She took a deep breath. It felt like her mind was drifting thinking on how things had changed so fast in her life. She had come to love the gigantic big house, that she now called home. It resembled an enchanted home like one she seen in an old Hollywood movie. The home, nestled in the San Juan Bautista Valley, was an exact replica of a Spanish mission, complete with a giant wrought iron gate to protect the estate from unwanted intrusions.

Her eyes shifted from the geese in the pond to admiring a covered walkway alive with a bright yellow Bougainvillea, named California Gold.

Camille thought about the conversation she had had with Desmond, the night before. Their conversations had always come easy for them. They had an easy-going relationship. But Camille had been aware there was a void between them. The chasm she knew had to be with whether or not it was time. She knew that babysitting Tiara's sons had stirred the interest within her. But she hadn't known that Desmond had been ready for them to start a family.

Camille was still staring off into space when she heard the bedroom door open. She looked up into the eyes of her husband, Desmond Garcia. She smiled softly. "I heard you getting up earlier and thought you'd gone for the day."

Desmond's handsome face smiled back at her, as he closed the distance between them.

"Honey, why are you still in your robe?" She asked.

Desmond shrugged, as he sat down on the bed beside her. "I couldn't leave without a little early morning loving," he grinned. "Besides, I thought maybe we could get started on making what we were talking about, last night."

Camille could see the excitement in Desmonds eyes and she heard the exuberance in his voice. She grinned softly. "Are you sure you want us to start a family, now? Right this moment?"

Desmond chuckled. "Woman, can't you tell by looking at the rising tidal wave under my robe." He guided her hand to the opening in his robe.

Camille's eyes sparkled and flashed with knowing. "Hmmm…", she moaned, as her hand explored his body.

Desmond kissed the side of her face. "I don't think we should think about having a baby. I think we should just do what comes naturally and see what happens. Besides, nothing gets me going first thing in the morning, like a little bit of loving from my loving wife."

Camille tilted her head and kissed him softly on his nose. "You know traffic on highway 101 is going to be crazy, if you don't get started," she said, with a teasing smile.

"This old world is cruel and hard, but it ain't half as bad, when I get a little extra something from you, first thing in the morning," he said kissing her.

She smiled wickedly. Yearning for the touch of him. "Oh, you mean like a little bit of early morning loving."

"Damn, woman I love you. You can read my mind," he moaned, as he slid kisses down her neck.

Camille moaned softly with pleasure and whispered. "You know when I woke up, I felt that something good, and hard was coming my way," she softly laughed. "A good hard stiff one, beats a cup of coffee first thing in the morning," she said, untying his robe and sliding her hand inside and pushing him back on the bed and straddling him.

With his mouth, Desmond caught a taut dark nipple in his mouth and sucked it deeply.

"Oui shit," Camille whimpered. "Yes, baby, momma likes!" She exclaimed as her hand clasped his penis and directed it towards the swollen lips of her vagina. Slowly she lowered herself over the head of his dick

"Damn, woman you are so wicked," Desmond swore, as his penis enjoyed the tight in-and-out motion as she worked her hips.

Finally, Desmond flipped Camille over on her back, feeling her about to come at any moment. "Feels good?"

"Yes, it feels real good," Camille whimpered.

"You want more," he teased.

"Yes!"

"What do you want? Say it," he said.

"I want you to come inside of me," Camille said wrapping her legs around him feeling the intense sensation of pure satisfaction consuming her. She felt a heighten sensation of her sense and then a strong smell engulfed her. Deep inside she felt extreme pleasure. Something new and different was happening she felt it deep within.

Chapter 4

Glenda D'Goodwrench, Scott Irishman-Jackson, Common and Fannie

It was Wednesday morning, in the old town of San Juan Bautista, California. The old picturesque town was the home of one of California's most famous mission. The mission is where the movie Vertigo was filmed. The town of San Juan Bautista was also where Glenda D'Goodwrench, and her husband Scott Irishman-Jackson, called home.

They lived on the second floor of an old rustic building on the corner of Main Street. The first floor housed the family's business, a bar. Their bar was famous for a drink that they called *Cadillac Margarita*, a drink served with an extra shot of tequila on the side.

The entrance way of the old rustic building had a banister railing, that some folks said, came to life when their fingertips touched the knotted twisting grapevines that looped and wrapped their way around the banister.

That morning, Scott Irishman-Jackson, sat at the end of the bar on a high stool with his eyes glued to a television set, while he busied himself with the crochet needle and yarn in his hands.

He concentrated as he counted the cadence of the crochet needle's movement. "Knit one, curl two, knit four, curl two," he softly sung to himself.

A jet-black cat sat on top of the television cabinet and scrutinized the man.

Suddenly the man stopped crocheting and shrieked. "Pinky are you about to have one of your color changing spells?" He inquired but didn't expect the cat to respond. "Well if you are will you please carry yourself off somewhere until the act is done? I'm trying to knit here."

As if she understood what the man had said, the cat purred loudly, and jumped off the television cabinet and scurried out of the room.

Instantly the soft tinkering bells chimed, signaling the front door had been opened.

"Welcome, come on in and sit for a while. My name is Scott Irishman-Jackson, and yes, I'm the proprietor," he said, not glancing up. "By the way, we are famous for our *Cadillac Margarita*s, and fresh strawberry is the premier flavor today. Would you care for one?"

"Yes, and I was anticipating a bowl of your fresh strawberries to eat as well. I understand they are the finest for miles around," an unusual sounding woman's voice carried across the room. She sounded like she came from far away.

Scott Irishman-Jackson looked up. The woman had wild jet black wavy hair that swung to her waist and she was wearing some unusual clothing, she reminded him of an angel. "Good day, Miss? Have a seat and I'll get you that bowl of fresh strawberries."

"My name is Fanny and I hear your wife Glenda makes some of the best tasting fresh blueberry muffins, as well. And I'll take some of those too, for my friend Common, if you don't mind," she hesitated. "Oh, and he'll have a strawberry margarita, as well."

At the mention of a friend named Common, Irishman-Jackson stopped what he was doing. He was sure he had only seen the woman enter.

"Sure thing, Ms. Fanny," he declared out loud.

"Sounds good, if you don't mind, we'll take a booth," Fanny announced.

"Sure, no worries," Irishman-Jackson spoke out strong and then silently said a prayer to himself in Gaelic as he gawked. *"Oir is leatsa an rìoghachd, agus an cumhachd, agus a'ghlòir, gu sìorraidh. Amen."*

It was the prayer words he'd often heard his Irish grandmother on his mother's side say when she realized she was coming up against a power greater than any she had ever known. He headed to the kitchen to put a batch of muffins in the oven.

Secretly, his eyes stole glances at the man the woman named Fanny had called Common. There wasn't anything common about him, in fact, Irishman-Jackson was certain he was some sort of wizard, sorcerer or worst a warlock. He shivered with his theories and wished he had not made Pinky the cat leave the room.

As if she had sensed his distress, Pinky the cat made her

appearance. Scott Irishman-Jackson smiled to himself when he saw
Pinky enter the kitchen and suddenly head straight to the bar. He
followed her and busied himself making their drinks.

He glanced out of the corner of his eye to see what Pinky was
up to. Her fur coat was a deep violet color as she eased close to
Common. Instantly, Pinky's fur changed to a vibrate majestic Gold
color as a purring growl swelled up in her throat as she turned, made
her exit and hurried up the staircase to the family's home above the
bar.

*"Good girl Pinky, you do that. You go and get the lady of the
house. She'll know what to do with these two,"* Scott Irishman-
Jackson, said to himself.

Loudly he cleared his throat. "Well, here are your drinks and
the bowl of strawberries. The muffins will be done soon, enjoy."

"I do love the gold and distressed-gold motif of your wall
décor. It adds an old-world charm and elegance to the place," Fanny
said.

Just then Glenda came down the staircase. "Yes, it does," she
said to her guest as she closed the distance between them. "Hello,
and welcome," she said as she made her way across the room. I'm
Glenda D'Goodwrench-Jackson, and you met my husband, Scott
Irishman-Jackson, he and I are the owners."

Pinky the cat, jumped up into Glenda's arms and she began
caressing her. Her rich full was still a majestic gold color that
looked luminous.

Glenda turned her attention. "By the way, I believe you've
met Pinky."

"Yes, I did, my name is Fanny, and this is my friend
Common."

Glenda watched Fanny like a hawk. "Well Fanny, you and
your friend Common are welcome, please enjoy your visit. May I
ask if your friend Common, is the one and only Common Ogun, the
Bokor?"

"Yes, Common is he," Fanny said. "He is of the Ogun
family from Haiti, Bokor. I believe you and I met a long time ago."

"Please sit down and join us," Glenda replied, as her eyes
widened and gave her a surprised look. She felt a wide tangle of
emotions. How had they met? She didn't remember. "Oh, I don't

recall meeting you."

Fanny smiled wide. "You and I were at a masquerade ball, when we first meet. It was the Tarragon Dark Moon Masquerade Ball, held in Oakland, at the Paramount Theater. That was a couple of years ago and I was wearing the silver and black long nose mask with the black angel wings," she laughed. "Bella Fire-Dragon introduced us."

Glenda's smile froze. She remembered that night at the Tarragon Dark Moon Masquerade Ball. She'd thought Bella Fire-Dragon had been playing a joke on her when she'd introduced her to Fanny, the fallen angel. "Oh, of course, I, remember, now."   She had forgotten their introduction. When Bella had introduced her to Fanny, the two had been joking about the man in the devil costume resembling the real thing.

Glenda thought back to that fateful night when Fanny walked up to her in black Angel winged costume, complete with long nose mask and Bella had joked making introductions, "Now *the lady walking towards us in the black angel wings costume, is none other than Ms. Fanny, the fallen angel. That means Glenda, that you and I have just met, Fanny the fallen Angel, her sidekick Common, and look here the devil, just walked by. Now our night is complete. All hell can break loose, let the party began! It's going to be one wild night of hocus pocus! Because the devil made us do it!" Bella yelled, laughing hysterically.*

Glenda shook out her thoughts remembering how they had all three laughed at Bella's joke. Finally, remembering she wasn't alone, she looked up at Fanny and gave her a tight smile.

"Oh, yes, now I truly remember and looks like I should sit down and have a chat with you and your friend Common," Glenda said, taking a seat across from Fanny.

"Yes, yes… You must," Fanny said. "Might we have those muffins you are famous for? Before we have our chat? Common is very hungry."

Glenda shook her head in agreement. Just as the oven timer dinged that the muffins were ready. "Jackson, darling, the oven timer just went off," she called out loudly. "Could you bring us the muffins?"

Jackson leaned his head out of the kitchen. "Sure, thing, my love, would you like me to brew you up a pot of tea?"

"Yes, my love," Glenda replied.

A few minutes later Jackson walked over to their table with the basket of fresh, piping hot muffins, sweet butter, and another bowl of strawberries.

"I'll just run along," Jackson replied, "Your pot of tea will be right out."

Fanny's dark brown eyes twinkled as she reached out a slim delicate hand and retrieved a muffin and setting her gaze on Glenda. "These muffins are delicious, and I think I'll have a cup of tea with you as well."

"What kind of tea will you be serving?" Common inquired, his voice carrying not one whit of criticism.

It was the first-time Glenda had heard Common utter a sound. She was fascinated by the tone of his speech. It sounded ancient and full of wisdom.

"It's a smooth black Taiwanese tea. It goes particularly well with the muffins," Glenda replied.

Just then Jackson settled the tray with the pot of tea and three cups on the table. He poured a cup of tea for their guest and then his wife Glenda. His eyes looked pleadingly into hers.

Glenda knew Jackson was letting her know he would be sitting in the kitchen listening to their conversation. She nodded and turned her attention back to her guest.

Common took a sip of his tea. "The Taiwanese black tea is smooth. I've tried it before. Have you heard of the Red-bush tea?" He asked but didn't wait for a response. "The best grow just north of Capetown, South Africa. If you haven't tried it. You must."

Glenda cocked her head to one side amazed that Common knew so much about tea. "As you say, I must try it."

"Okay," Fanny said. "Enough about tea. You do know that there is a reason we are here?"

Glenda nodded. She wasn't a bit surprised when Fanny stopped the tea chitchat. She'd seen the serious look on her face.

"Anyway," Fanny went on. "You and your friends were approached by a man named Delmar Devereaux for help. But you must know that his ailment is a product of his former life."

Glenda nodded understanding. "Yes, Delmar sort of briefed

us on the matter that he and the young woman were soul mates in a past life."

Common shook his head. "I must state for the record that when I speak of Delmar, I am speaking of his ancestor who committed the deed. You see I must say that to tell that a crime of passion was carried out, over a hundred years ago, by Delmar's ancestor. Delmar was told this, but he did not tell you and your friends the truth, of what took place in his past life."

"But perhaps his ears could not bear it," Fanny added shaking her head.

Common nodded. "Mankind's romantic notions can set in motions powers of the unforeseen. Throughout time, the romantic union between man and woman is sacred. For the union is meant to serve more than just animalistic drive for sex and pleasure. Its purpose is meant to provide the capability of the lovers to evolve their state of being from the sphere of flesh to a greater realm of existence through the correct operation of the sexual high energy."

"My goodness, Common is correct," Fanny exclaimed. "But Delmar's ancestor used it to destroy a beautiful innocent all because she did not possess the dowry money his family had expected as payment for their marriage."

"What? I don't understand." Glenda cut in.

Fanny's eyes widen as she continued. "The young woman thought that since she did not have the dowry money promised, the marriage contract was void and she was fine with that because it is said she did not want to marry Delmar's relative anyway. But once Delmar's ancestor learned that the lovely young woman had not the dowry money his family required and because he was so infatuated with her, he cast out a devilish scheme to possess her."

Common nodded his eyes steady and unwavering. "And he carried out the deed," he added. "He raped her and when her family went to the law to protest. Delmar's ancestor conveniently found an outstanding gambling debt that the girl's father had made and he quickly brought it up so that he had power. Power to persuade the law to act against the girls family and he had the law sieze the young woman as as payment for her father's debt. The young woman was turned over in servitude to Delmar's ancestor to pay off her father's debt."

"Oh, the trauma she suffered at the hands of Delmar's ancestor," Fanny shrieked. "It took its toll on the young woman and she hung herself before the birth of her baby."

Common gave a dazed somewhat sad smile. "Once the girl's family discovered her lifeless body they placed a curse on Delmar's ancestor," he said, as his voice became mute.

Fanny exchanged glances with Glenda. "Common stops talking from time to time like that, especially when he feels a pull on his energies."

Suddenly Common grabbed Fanny's hand. "We have to tell Glenda the truth. This is only the story that came down from the telling. What we are saying is that it might not be all that there was."

"What do you mean?" Glenda inquired

"That story might not be all the truth," Fanny declared.

"For there is always two sides to every story," Common said. "And sometimes the truth is buried deep."

Fanny looked from Common's face back to Glenda. "But we are trying to discover what the truth is."

"I know we are trying but our words are not enough," Common replied, releasing her hands and rubbing the palms of his hands together.

Fanny studied Common's face. "There is no sense in avoiding what has to be done. Especially if it helps makes sense of it all. I'm sure Glenda won't mind a little conjuring."

He turned and looked at Glenda. "I think I have something that will show you what we are truly dealing with here. If you don't mind."

"Of course, I don't mind," Glenda said. "If it'll help."

"I'm a little out of practice," Common replied, as he sprayed the palms of his hands out in the center of the table and dropped stones that looked like old bones. Instantly, multi-colored sparks of light danced up as he chanted softly to himself and then finally said out loud. "Beauty is the light that comes forth from our soul. Some can see this light, others cannot, but it is always there… Be it in this time, this place or another time and place. Show us the truth unseen…"

Common stretched his arms wide across the table and waited and then said. "A day, a moon, a hundred lifetimes, bring forth the man, who once was Delmar Devereaux."

Vaporizing mist swirl until colorful images appeared and spun out and around, coalesced into the form of what had been a man.

A shadow he was, Glenda thought glancing back at the form of the man. It faced her and spun forward and stared back into her eyes. As she stared she saw the depths of pain furrow his brows and reek from its shadowy fog. "Can you speak spirit?"

"I can, and I must," its voice squeezed out in a cry of pain. "I walk back to this earth to right the wrong done many years ago, for I have been waiting for her many life times."

Glenda leaned closer. "Who are you?" She asked the question out of habit. Not expecting what was to come. The atmosphere changed.

The spirit stared sadly back at her. A singeing loneliness filled the air. It was cold and filled with agony.

"I am he, who wronged the woman who carried my child," his voice cried. "Back then in the old times and now. For my foolish kinsman, Delmar, shares my spirit and he has made a devil's bargain that will repeat what was done, in the past. And if I don't stop him. Our sons will be lost to us forever and on my oath, I will not let this happen, I cannot let this happen," the spirit's voice cried and then cracked, coughed, and his vapor body of fog almost collapsed into a heap.

Glenda trembled for a moment afraid he was gone until seconds later, the fog assembled itself back into a man's form. It was then that she saw that it really did resemble Delmar Devereaux completely, right down to the dark hair and dark eyes and the razor thin moustache.

His body shifted. "Forgive, it takes a lot of energy to walk this earth. Now, where was I?" He asked fixing his gaze on Glenda. "Mistress Glenda D'Goodwrench, I need your help. For you and your friends can help me, please! I beg you."

Glenda was frozen by the sad cold stare as the spirit of Delmar's eyes held her's. Her heart pounded in her chest, "Well, I guess it could be. I will do my best to help ..."

"Oh, thank you! Thank you!" The spirited interrupted her finishing her. "I knew you would agree to help me," he replied moaning and rocking from side to side.

The spirit looked around as if taking in his surroundings for the very first time., "Common, I really must thank you for helping me to make this journey. Please forgive my cries and moans, it takes a lot of energy to walk this earth. I really should be going, I don't belong here."

Glenda stole a glance and Common at realized something was wrong. Common looked like a shadow of his former self. It was her first clue that something was wrong. Her next clue was that the cold air surrounding them was starting to dissipate.

Glenda shifted her weight bracing herself to be alert if anything should happen. She didn't have long to wait. Just then a crack of thunder sounded loud and energy swirl. The lights in the bar flickered on and off.

The foggy mist that was Delmar's ancestor levitated and rose high as if a vortex was opening above him.

Common grimaced and shifted as if transformed. By an ionizing charge of energy. He braced himself and said through gritted teeth. "You have not told us all, spirit of Delmar's ancestor. I will let the vortex take you, if you do not tell us the truth!"

"Wait, no!" the spirit cried. "I will be lost forever if the vortex takes me."

Common transfixed his magic and power and instantly the vortex was gone.

"Nice trick," Glenda muttered.

"Speak spirit!" Common commanded.

"When the woman that was Tiara's ancestor discovered she was pregnant, she went to see Eve Laveau, a practicing rootworker, conjure woman, whom she told she needed a powerful spell, one that would get her revenge on Delmar's relative. The conjure woman's spell was so powerful, it can only be described as a curse and it resonates today."

The Spirit of Delmar's ancestor coughed hysterically. "I feel the realms are unstable…"

"Spirit!" Common interrupted him.

"I will finish! I will finish!" The Spirit blurted. "The only way my relative can break the curse is to go on a quest to find the ingredients that must be used to break it. But he cannot make the journey along. He must be accompanied by a descendant of Marie Laveau's family."

"Why?" Glenda blurted and repeated. "Why must that be so?"

"Don't you see?" The Spirit asked but didn't wait for an answer. "The conjure woman Eve, was a distant cousin of the first Marie…"

"Marie Laveau?" Glenda interrupted.

The Spirit coughed fiercely. "I cannot… The realms are unstable."

"Oh, my goodness. You are growing faint Spirit," Glenda stated. Glenda was sure that the spirit had depleted his energy. The coughing fit he was having was proof. She was just about to put an end to his visit.

"I can feel what you are thinking Glenda, but he's alright," Common said as his expression grew hard.

He sent a concentrated icy stare at the spirit. "Now finish telling her spirit!"

"As you command Common," the spirit said. "Glenda my dear, I'm afraid it wasn't just chance luck that I choose to present myself to you. You are best friends with Nona, and she has a great untapped gift that will be very useful. It is your friend Nona that must help my descendant, Delmar."

"Oh, my!" Glenda blurted. "Nona…She is a Laveau?"

"Yes, she is," the Spirit said. "Nona is a true direct descendant of Marie Laveau and she is the only one who can break the powerful spell her ancestor unleashed on my ancestor."

The spirit's eyes were wide with fright. "The realms are unstable, something to do with Mercury retrograde, I must leave. But before I do. Know that Nona and Delmar must go to the San Mateo Historic Museum in Redwood City at stroke of bewitching hour, no earlier, no later. Be sure to tell Nona and Delmar before they take the journey, for it is here that they will discover their first clue of the needed ingredient and where to find it."

The Spirit stood quietly for a moment. "Be sure to stress to them that they must obtain the items needed in the order that they are listed, to break the curse. A map will be provided and it will only become visible as each item is obtained."

A thunderous clap sounded loud and explosive as a shimmering light descended over them.

The room shook all around them, as glasses and bottles vibrated on shelves.

A crack of thunder sounded loud then the utterly inexplicable happened. In the center of the ceiling a storm raged as the center of the storm opened and an object birthed from the eye of the storm and hurled its way falling free. It landed right at Glenda's feet.

All at once Common lowered his hands and Glenda felt the air suck out of the room with a suction power so great she wondered why it didn't leave the room looking like a tornado had hit it.

The spirt coughed fiercely and disappeared.

Glenda bent down and picked up the object. It was a high-quality parchment paper scroll. Carefully, she opened it. Slowly invisible writing appeared. It was the map the spirit had spoke of.

Written in a deep blood red color at the bottom of the parchment it stated boldly. *"Only a descendant of Marie Laveau, may touch any of the items needed to break the spell, or the curse cannot be broken."*

Chapter 5

TIARA, ERIS AND CAMILLE

With a glance at the mirror, Camille pouted her lips and reached her hand to the tight extra-large hair roller at the base of her neck, loosed it and ran her fingers through the loose curly waves of her cinnamon red highlighted hair. She swung her head. The effect was mesmerizing as a full loose cinnamon red highlighted curl dipped provocatively at her cheekbone emphasizing the elegance of her almond-shaped eyes.

Eris and Tiara exchanged glances.

"You look like you're ready to go home and seduce Desmond," Tiara teased.

"If she isn't, she ought to," Eris said tersely. "That look is first grade come and get it, daddy."

Tiara shrugged. "Your turn Eris," she murmured, rolling her eyes. "Show us what your new hairdo looks like, take off that scarf."

Eris grabbed the ends of the scarf that was tied so precisely on her head and slowly pulled the satin material from her head and with her free hand fluffed the fringed layers of her new bangs. Brilliant wild rose red colored hair cascade from the satin scarf.

Gone were the precision cut temple-to-temple bangs she had been known for. They had been replaced with softer fringe and feather bangs that were elegantly styled.

Camille let out a sigh. "Wow, Eris, that looks really suits you. You did a complete overhaul," she hesitated. "I mean it really becomes you."

Tiara pretended not to notice. She ran her fingers through her custom bronze blonde streaked long hair. Over the years, she had spent large sums money making sure her hair color was as real looking as possible. "It looks alright Eris, but why such a change in color? Looks like you back on the market trying to catch anything but a cold," she shrugged.

"Jealous are we," Eris said, faking politeness.

Tiara jerked her head up. "Jealous of you? Never! I'm just looking out for you, I thought you already had a man," she said with a sharp edge to her voice.

Eris' voice rose. "Of course, I do," she said, cloyingly sweet. "But I want to look extra romantic and sexy for Ethan. A woman should always spice herself up, extra special for her man."

Tiara hated it when Eris rubbed it in how she had a man, and she didn't. Eris was right, she was jealous. She hated it. After having her sons, she realized just how empty and incomplete her life was. Oh, her sons were her joy, but they were also a constant reminder of how their father had treated her, and treated them. It was like having them brought up old childhood memories of her own, exposing the little girl that was once her and seeing what she at the time had thought was her father abandoning them. Only to learn, it was her mother always running away from her father, when he wouldn't let her have her way.

"Tiara...Tiara! Are you alright?" Camille inquired.

Camille's soft comforting voice woke Tiara from her thoughts. "Yes... I'm fine. As a matter of fact, I was just thinking why am I sitting in this beauty salon with a couple of old attached women. When I could be taking advantage of that all-day babysitter I have and go out into the world and meet someone?"

"Someone, don't you mean, Zack?" Camille asked.

Tiara laughed bitterly. "Zack who?" She asked, begrudgingly

"You know perfectly well, I mean Zackary Vaughn, the guy you've been seeing," Camille replied.

Camille and Eris looked at each other. Eris gave her a look and then reached for a comb and pretended to adjust a stray strand of hair. Camille knew what that look Eris was giving her meant. She was being selected to play the bad cop. She took a deep breath. "So, Tiara, what happened to Zack?"

"He had to go," Tiara said matter-of-factly. "I kicked his ass to the curb. Imagine the nerve of him, telling me he felt I should let Delmar see my sons."

Eris laughed and shook her head. "The no-good sinner. I bet you had him sweating like a sinner in church when you kicked him to the curb. But first I know you rode that pony hard one last time," she said giving her a sneer as their eyes held.

Tiara barely heard her, her thoughts raced as she released a heavy sigh. Over the years, she had grown a thick skin towards Eris and her fake politeness.   She knew what Eris really thought of her. Her words had been etched in her mind for years now. *"You act all regal and refined and we all know you're no lady. You know you really just a sex-addict."*

Tiara was startled when she felt a light touch on her arm. She looked from the hand patting arm to the face. Camille winked back at her.

"Are you alright, Tiara? Eris didn't mean to upset you," Camille's soft eyes beamed back at her.

Embarrass me? Tiara thought, as she took a deep breath and shook out her thoughts. "Sure, I'm good. I just really need some alone time today. You know what I mean?"

Tiara didn't wait for Camille to respond as she hurried to the door and made her exit.

Chapter 6

DELMAR DEVEREAUX

☐ Delmar stood at his bedroom window and gawked, reveling in the late afternoon sun and appreciating a glass of California Cabernet Sauvignon. He admired the view of the Pacific Ocean his bedroom afforded him. The Monterey coast line was beautiful this time of year, he thought taking in the view it gave of Wild Cove to the south.

He took a sniff of the glass of wine he held. The vintage wine was noted to be one of the best per his favorite magazine, The Wine Advocate. He was just about to finished his glass when he saw a car pulling into his driveway.

"Holy crap! What do they want?" he said under his breath when he saw the three ladies getting out of the car.

He was glad today wasn't his housekeeper's day off. He shuffled over to his intercom system and asked Daisy to show the ladies to the patio.

A short time later, Delmar was glad he had suggested bringing the three ladies to his back patio. His patio offered a spectacular coastal view of the Monterey Bay. With the lateness of the day, the evening sun setting had added to the conversation of his three guest, he thought as he observed them from a hidden distance.

The three ladies stood at the railing of the redwood deck, babbling and laughing at the view.

"Their home is not too far from here. But I have not seen them for years, the family's last name was Dragonstone, they gave some of the best parties back in the day. I heard the son may have sold off the place," Glenda said, making chitchat.

Nona nodded. "I remember them," she added, "The mother was part of Ancient Ways."

Consuela shook her head. "Yes, she was part of the Berkley Chapter. She had the most stunning head of silver-gray hair."

Nona was just about to open her mouth as she looked up and noticed their host returning.

She touched Glenda's arm. "Our host, Delmar has come back."

The three ladies turned and watched Delmar close the distance between them.

"I'm so glad you let us enjoy your view," Consuela said, with a Spanish accent.

"Yes, and we must thank you for your hospitality," Nona added. "The lite supper of Salad and Fresh Grilled Salmon was excellent."

"Yes, it was," Glenda nodded. "But, I think it is time for us to tell you why we have come,"

"Perhaps we could all have a strong drink before you do Glenda," Nona suggested. "I know I could use something stronger than ice tea."

Delmar smiled. "Nona, you and I are on the same page. Can I offer you, ladies, a glass of California Cabernet?"

"I'll have a lowball glass of Bourbon, if you got it," Nona replied.

"No worries, I sure can. You think like me, I would love something stronger," Delmar laughed. "In fact, I can provide you all with your choice of hard liquor."

"Then I'll have the Patrón," Consuela giggled.

"A snifter of Patrón Añejo, coming right up," Delmar said. "And you Glenda?"

"I'll have the same, a snifter of Patrón Añejo will set me up just right," Glenda replied.

Delmar nodded, as he strolled back inside.

A half-hour later, Delmar returned with their drinks and a tray of filled with sliced lemons, and pineapples along with tortilla chips, pico de gallo, guacamole and Mexican Avocado Bruschetta.

A while later, after devouring their drinks Glenda cleared her throat. "Well, this is as fine a moment as any."

"Yes, and look how nice a night this is turning out to be. Why the moon and stars have astonished us with a visit," Consuela said vociferously, staring up at the sky.

Nona walked over to the railing of the redwood deck and noticed how the coast of Monterey had become shrouded in darkness so rapidly after the sunset. She took a deep breath and closed her eyes and noted how the air smelled funny.

"I'm sure you were wondering why we paid you a visit today, Delmar?" Glenda asked.

Nona opened her eyes and shook out her thoughts when she heard Glenda speak. She walked back over to their small group.

"Yes, I did," he said.

"Well, it seems one of your," Glenda hesitated. "Distant relatives paid us a visit and the news he brought ..."

"Distant relative..." Delmar shrugged. "But, I don't recall..."

"She means your ancient distant relative," Nona interrupted.

"Yes, an ancient and very dead one," Consuela added to the conversation.

"I see," Delmar said, taking a sip of his Bourbon. "Are you sure it was one of my ah...Ancient distant relatives? You know many people look alike."

"Oh, yes," Glenda said, "The family resemblance is very strong in you. He even had your dark hair and dark eyes and that razor thin mustache you love to sport."

Delmar couldn't believe what he was hearing. He thought they couldn't be serious. He grinned mischievously. "Isn't that a hoot, my ancient relative who looked like me, paid you a visit. I bet he thinks I turned out pretty bad, huh," he chuckled and blurted out laughing. "This is hilarious! Did he mention anything about my kicking my babies momma to the curb?"

Nona pressed her lips into a frown. "It's nothing to joke about, Delmar. This is serious. You disrupted the past and now you are making a mockery of your future."

"Disrupte the past? Woman? All I did was betrayal the mother of my children's trust and loyalty and I came to you to help me fix that!" Delmar interjected.

Glenda was careful to keep her face expressionless. "But we've learned something Delmar, don't you see? Something very important."

With a quick nod, Consuela blurted with a trace of impatience in her voice. "Glenda's right Delmar, that is why we are here."

For some strange reason, Delmar felt the hairs on the back of his neck stand up. A pungent smell dominated the air. His eyes peered up at the moon. The sky was murky, black, and the moon was full. He sensed a weird chill and something deep within propelled him to immediately walked over to the patio cabinet and pulled out a few blankets retrieve them and then presented them to the three ladies.

"Here, these will keep you warm," Delmar said, after choosing one of the blankets and draping it around his shoulder.

Nona was the first to shake out her blanket and take a really good look at it. "These are not blankets. I mean in the sense of the word, yes, they are blankets. But just look at the fine stitches. This is an heirloom. Down south, we call them quilts."

Glenda shook her head. "Indeed, they are. This quilt feels like something my grandmother would have made."

"I know this pattern," Consuela added.

"Yes, I do too," Nona replied.

"It's the interlocking circles," the three ladies said in unison, as three sets of eyes turned to Delmar.

"Delmar," Nona said. "Where did you obtain these?"

"Oh, from some distant relative. I believe they were my grandmothers. All I know is that I was forbidden to get rid of them," he joked.

The three ladies got quiet and stared back at him. Suddenly, a strange darkness descended upon them. Their heads turned looking around them. It took them a minute to realize what was happening. As a strange fog engulfed the patio deck.

"Do you feel that?" Nona whispered.

"What the hell is going on?" Delmar asked, feeling bewildered as the hairs on his neck were joined by goosebumps.

"Shhhhh! Be quiet, everyone!" Glenda cautioned. "And whatever you do, keep your quilt wrapped around you."

It got real quiet and then, the mist thickened around them. It was as if the vapor surrounding them was developing into a portal. There was a great silence and then the air felt like something was transitioning and shifting and that was when the spirit came out of the fog.

"Eeeeeee! Heeeeee! Deeee! "Passing from one plane to another is never an easy transition," the spirit coughed. "Delmar! Delmar! Is that you?" The spirit demanded.

Delmar looked at the spirit coming his way and thought his ugly ways had finally landed him in purgatory.

Delmar bared his teeth like a dog getting ready to growl "Who are you and how do you know my name?"

The spirit frowned. "You know me Delmar, a part of me has existed within you since the day of your birth. You are me as I am you, always."

The spirit descended upon him and Delmar's eyes focused. He trembled, and a little clicking sound came out of him as he tried to remain composed. The spirit looked just like him, it was uncanny. "And who are you?"

"In a previous life, I am you, Delmar," the spirit said.

Delmar spun around so fast, he almost collided with Nona. He gasped out. "Nona! Glenda! Consuela! What kind of sick joke is this?"

The truth had to be told. Nona grabbed Delmar by the shoulders and spun him back around and tucked his quilt tightly around him. "Delmar... Meet your Ancient descendant," Nona said making introductions. "He's your relative like he said."

Nona took a step forward. "By the way spirit, you never told us your name."

"I too, am named Delmar, believe it or not," the spirit replied. "It is good that you all are wearing the interlocking circles for protection. Sometimes other energies take advantage of the portal being open and travel through. I have tried to be careful but…"

His words peaked Glenda's interest as she suddenly interrupted. "Did something travel through the portal with you?"

"I cannot know for sure, but I felt something," he put his hand to his brow as if he was thinking. He shifted as if shaking out his thoughts. "No, I can't feel anything, perhaps I may have been wrong."

"Spirt why are you here?" Glenda inquired.

The spirit laughed as if the laughter was lodged deep in his chest before expelling out of his mouth. "Why to help convince my relative to go on his Quest!"

The spirit laughed out loud as if he told a joke. He closed the distance between him and Delmar. "Nothing like putting a little bit of fear in the living to get them to know you mean business."

Chapter 7

TIARA & DELMAR

The next day Delmar woke early, he couldn't sleep. When he looked at the invitation for the Annual Music of the Heart, annual gala benefit, on his desk the day before, he realized what he had to do. He dressed swiftly and headed for his office.

The event was A Musical Feast, an elegant evening of dining and dancing with a very special performance by members of the Amazing Blazing Gospel Singers and Orchestra, at the Fairmont Hotel in San Jose, it was Tiara's favorite. He knew she couldn't afford the tickets on her own and getting her to come would be easy.

At precisely nine o'clock that morning, He watched as his secretary pretended she was calling from the Annual Music Heart Committee and reached out to Tiara by telephone. She'd informed her that she was the winner of complimentary tickets. Hearing Tiara's shouts of joy, over the speakerphone assured him she would be at that night's event.

He'd winked back at his secretary Marva, and gave her a high five before he left the office.

***

Later that same night, across town, Tiara Blake couldn't believe her good luck, her old friend Eris had agreed to babysit the twins for her.

Since the moment she had arrived, she felt like her adrenaline had kicked into high gear.   This event was just what she needed to make her feel alive again.

"Tiara Blake is that you?"

Tiara instantly recognized the voice. It was an ex-beauty queen, Isla Wickham, and she was quickly closing the gap between them.

"Hi Isla, long time no see," Tiara blurted, feigning to be happy to see her.

"Oh, Tiara, you declare that so charmingly, when we both know we despise each other's guts," Isla, uttered in her sexy hoarse voice. "Come, walk with me to the bar, I'll get us some drinks."

"Okay," Tiara responded. "I could use one."

After wasting an unpleasant half hour with Isla sipping on her glass of wine and performing small talk. Tiara was wondering what Isla was thinking when she suddenly grew silent. She didn't have long to wait.

Isla threw back her glass of wine and finished it. "Well, now that I finished my glass of courage, it's confession time," she declared, softening her voice and leaning in close.

"Pardon, me? What did you say?"

"You heard me loud and clear," Isla rebutted. "Damn, you are still a beautiful-looking heifer, even after those twins of yours ripped through your body."

Tiara gawked back at her catlike eyes and realized Isla was still resentful of her. "Jealous? Aren't we Isla," she snickered, ruefully. "By the way you need to lay off the wine."

"Yes, I am very jealous. Especially seeing you wearing that off the shoulder, clingy red gown you are in right now. I mean who helped you pick that out. I need your stylist phone number."

Tiara giggled. "Wow, you are being honest tonight, Isla."

"I should lay off the wine. I told you it's my truth serum. This is my second glass, right?" Isla asked.

"No, it was your fourth," Tiara responded. "But, who's counting."

Isla flung back her hair. "You realize I am jealous of you Tiara," she declared. "You've made two beautiful sons, and you got your body back. I bet if their daddy could see you now, he'd demand to take you home and rip that dress off you. You realize that man had a thing for you from the minute I introduced you," she added giggling shaking her head. "Damn, I want a man to rip my dress off me."

Tiara grimaced at the thought of Delmar Devereaux, she had forgotten Isla Wickham, knew about her relationship with Delmar. In fact, Isla was correct, she had been the one to introduce her to Delmar. From the moment she had shaken hands with Delmar that fateful night many years ago their electrical chemistry had sealed her to him. She recalled how Isla's eyes had looked at her after as she smirked and said. *"My... My... That is the real love at first sight stuff if I ever saw it. I thought I was going to have to get the jaws of life to get that man to stop shaking your hand," she laughed.*

"I see that look you have in your eyes, Tiara. You are still in love with Delmar, admit it."

"I like Delmar, Tiara said to herself. Maybe a slight too much... Oh, my... I like him a lot, in love with Delmar?" Tiara thought back to that night a long time ago, when she first met Delmar. A warm tingling coursed through Tiara's body as she thought about him. She wondered if he felt the same. Tiara eased a loose strand of hair behind her ear and shook out her thoughts. She prayed Isla couldn't read her mind.

Isla touched Tiara's arm. "Earth to Tiara, girl are you in there. Looks like you off in daydream land."

Tiara had to press her lips together to keep from telling Isla her thoughts.

Isla's giggled and smiled in pleasure. "Girlfriend, it's confession time. If Delmar ever gave me the time of day, I wouldn't care if that scum bag baby daddy of yours didn't wife me, because I would still do my wifey duties just to ride that handsome man," she barked out with laughter.

Tiara ignored Isla as she took a sip of her wine. She had forgotten Isla had a big crush on Delmar.

Isla gulped down her glass of wine and gesture for the bartender to make her another one.

Tiara seized the opportunity to stroll a few steps away from her.

"Hey Tiara, wait up," Isla called. "You're not annoyed about what I said?"

"Isla, why are you telling me this?" Tiara inquired with a jeer.

"Cause, I wanted you to know I found Delmar attractive. But I can see you're uncomfortable with my saying I'd sleep with Delmar if he asked me too."

Tiara grimaced. "I… I just can't believe you would say..."

Isla interrupted. "What that I'd sleep with him? Came on Tiara, you're a big girl. Why don't you just accept you've still got feelings for Delmar?"

"Bullshit!"

Isla shook her head. "I can see that you just still aren't ready to admit that you do. Don't take too long discovering the truth Tiara, about your feeling for him or you may miss out on loving that man."

Tiara felt like an idiot standing there having this discussion with Isla. She compressed her lips together to keep from telling Isla off. She was certain Isla wanted Delmar all to herself and the thought made her mad. She was just about to open her mouth with a comeback.

"Speaking of the devil, there's Delmar," Isla said, waving her hand, in his direction, getting his attention.

Tiara peered over the rim of her wineglass and saw Delmar walking over.

"Good evening Isla and Tiara," Delmar said, closing the gap between them.

Isla cleared her throat loudly. "Hello Delmar, my… My, don't you look extra handsome tonight," she declared letting her eyes roam up and down his body.

Tiara stopped and stared. She knew other women reacted to Delmar just like Isla was acting. Isla's behavior was typical because Delmar was a gorgeous man with his exquisitely cut hair curling slightly at the nape of his strong muscled neck.

Delmar walked over and gave Isla a brief hug. "So, do you," he replied, as he drew away unexpectedly and swept past her walking in close to Tiara.

"Tiara, what a surprise seeing you here tonight," Delmar said, eyeing her with hot eyes, from head to toe, a slight, twisted smile on his beautiful face. "You look marvelous! Red is your color."

Isla wasn't offended, she knew that look in Delmar's eyes, he was a man on a mission and he's radar had found his target.

"How are you doing, Delmar?" Tiara said, stepping away from him with swiftness.

"I'm good, Tiara," he said, with a nervous grin.

Isla eyed Tiara and uttered loudly. "Oh, yeah, Tiara, I have to get going, I'm late for that thing, I told you about," she declared, as she turned to make her exit.

"Hey wait, Isla," Tiara called. "Where did you say you were going?"

"You know that thing?" Isla called over her shoulder, as she sashayed across the room.

Tiara felt like an idiot, she detested being left behind with Delmar. It was at that moment that she recognized a peculiar floral scent and as the music from the main dance floor of the Regency Ballroom, became intense.

All at once Tiara looked up into Delmar's face. He had a curious look in his eyes. The glint in his eyes was so exquisitely strange, irresistibly seductive and powerful.

"Damn," she announced, glancing down at her empty glass. "I could really use a drink."

Delmar reached for her hand, took it and tucked her arm securely around his, making certain she couldn't escape. "Ahhhh, Then the lady shall have whatever she desires. Come, follow me."

"Right?" Tiara shrugged, trying her best to ignore him until she saw Isla's looking at her from the top of the staircase. She could have sworn Isla was mouthing the words to her to *behave*.

Tiara felt her emotions do a tailspin. She struggled hard not to expose what she was actually feeling. If she wasn't dressed to the nines, she would stroll over to Isla and whack the smirk off her face. It was an empowering moment when she realized she was the one, clutching the arm of the man they both wanted. It was at that moment that Tiara decided she'd make Isla feel jealous.

Tiara clung to Delmar's arm for the sake of Isla's eyes. She leaned in close and whispered. "Delmar why don't we go someplace private so that we can talk?"

"Sweetness, you are reading my mind."

Chapter 8

A Fling

Three hours later, Tiara felt like she was the center of attention under the spotlight, as she continued dancing in high heels and loving how good she looked all dressed up in her formal evening dress, on the dance floor of the Regency Ballroom. She couldn't believe she had been in Delmar Devereaux's company for the past three hours and neither one of them had started an argument.

The music came to an end, and she stopped breathless and took a step back. He stepped forward closing the gap between them.

"Oh, how you look beautiful dancing. Your eyes sparkle like a Goddess," Delmar said.

"This Goddess could certainly use an ice-cold drink with some liquor in it."

"As the lady commands," Delmar said, strolling over to the bar.

Tiara barely had enough time to fan herself before Delmar suddenly appeared by her side and put a drink in her hand.

The chilled blued colored cocktail had a cherry with a lime twist on top that Tiara quickly devoured before taking a big gulp of her drink.

"Mmmm, this is tasty. What's in it?" She inquired.

"That's 901 Silver tequila, blue curacao, lemon-lime soda and sweet and sour mix," he said.

Tiara leaned back against him. "Mmmm, momma likes," she answered, shifting to glance up at him. "Thank you, Delmar, for a wonderful evening."

The drink Delmar had given her was making her feel good, it went down so smoothly and made her feel relaxed from head to toe. She stared back into his eyes. She felt like she could stare into them all night. He looked perfect with his dark hair glistening in the dim light. She could scarcely believe this moment was real. It seemed so surreal like as she remembered that since the twins had been born she had wished a thousand times that he had held her. Abruptly she shook out her thoughts and took a step back.

That strange floral scent engulfed the air. Tiara wondered where it was coming from. A cold breeze of air surrounded her, and she shivered.

Delmar reached over and pulled her close so fast she literally fell against him. His kiss wasn't rough or angry but filled with passion. He tasted so good she wanted more, and she took it.

Delmar lifted his hands and cupped her face. The look on his face was intense as his fingers ran wildly over her face. "Come upstairs with me," he murmured, whispering in her ears.

His labored breathing told her he was serious. She felt the bulge straining his zipper and felt her heart skip a beat as she arched up against him.

Tiara couldn't seem to say no as she shook her head yes and wondered if it was appropriate for her to agree so fast. "You have a room here? Tonight?" she asked, amazed that the questions tumbled out of her mouth.

Delmar was already tugging her toward the elevator. His mind was filled with raging thoughts. He wanted Tiara badly, but he also had other motives. He hoped that after their night together she would see what he was doing was the best thing for all of them and then he remembered the twins as they entered the elevator and smiled. Soon they could all be a family.

Delmar seized the moment to forcefully kiss her as his hands traced down her body.

Tiara was game. "Easy now big daddy let's get to our room, my feet are killing me in these high heels."

As they entered Delmar's suite the first thing Tiara did was kick off her shoes. As she gave Delmar a piercing sexy expression that told him what she wanted. She stood there spellbound. She felt like she couldn't move. "Help me get out of this dress," she murmured in a sexy hoarse voice.

The expression on her face was all he needed to fuel his desire.

Tiara stood there and felt her clothes being gently removed from her body. Through a froggy gazed she noticed Delmar's face glowing with pleasure as he slowly removed her clothes.

Delmar's huge hands were warm as he pressed his bare-naked skin against hers. Somehow along the way Delmar had managed to remove his clothes.

Tiara could feel his erection against her bare skin as she gave into her need for sexual gratification. She reached down and grabbed his cock and squeezed. "You're good and hard already, Delmar," she purred.

"That's how you want it, right, beautiful?" he asked, huskily.

He gently slid down her to her abdomen to the mound between her legs. His tongue found her sweet spot.

Tiara moaned, spreading her legs wide as he pulled his face harder against it. "Ahhhh… Shhhhh. Oh yes, I'm feeling it!

"Feels good?" He murmured.

Tiara blurted. "Hell, yeah!"

"You want more?" He asked, teasingly.

"Yes, you know how I like you to give it to me."

"Then say what I want to hear," he ordered.

"Your loving is wicked," she moaned. "I want you inside me!"

Instantly Delmar rose and grabbed Tiara by the buttocks lifting her in the air and carrying her to the bed.

Twin moans filled the air as he slid pumping his cock inside her, Tiara felt her body exploding in sexual ecstasy as he rode her.

***

Early that morning, Tiara woke feeling elated in a warm and comfortable bed, last night had been amazing and she couldn't help but smile into her pillow as she remembered it.

Last night, Delmar's passionate lovemaking had brought tears to her eyes. She didn't have to tell him how to handle his business. He had predicted her every move.

She sat up in bed and let her gaze take in the room. When she had arrived last night, the room had been dark. She had never been in a room like this. A domed, glass room covered the roof and made the room feel like an atrium complete with tropical plants. One whole wall was glass and behind it, she could see cool, sweet water bathing pool. It looked like a tropical paradise.

Tiara got out of bed, naked, and headed toward the bathing pool. She debated looking for her clothes when she spotted a robe sitting in a chair.

When she heard the door of the suite opening, she marched in, robe in hand. "Delmar where have you been? --Oh!"

"Room service! I'm sorry miss, Mr. Devereaux, told me to come right in and set up breakfast. He said that you were still sleeping," the attendant replied, without glancing at Tiara's nude body.

Hastily, Tiara put on her robe and inhaling the aroma of fresh black coffee. "No worries. Do you know where Mr. Devereaux is now?"

"No, Miss, sorry I don't," the attendant answered, putting the finishing touches on the table he'd just assembled for two.

The attendant headed for the door. "By the way, Miss, there is no need to tip me, Mr. Devereaux took care of that before I arrived."

When the attendant left, Tiara knew as good a time as any take a shower. She headed down the hall to the bathroom.

She found a dressing area laid out with new clothes in her size there were a couple of dresses, jeans, tops, underwear and sandals all in her size. Delmar had even provided toiletries, some cosmetics, and a toothbrush. She smiled as she stepped into the shower.

Twenty minutes later, feeling comfortable in a pair of jeans, a fuchsia blouse, and sandals, she headed back into the main room and went straight to the table the waiter had laid out earlier.

Instantly, her hand went to the fresh pot of coffee and she poured herself a cup. She stared at the incredible array of dishes he laid out. There was enough food to feed an army. There was a tray of smoked salmon, French toast, fresh strawberries, blueberries and sliced peaches looked appetizingly appealing in a crystal truffle dish. Eggs Benedict sat warming in its own chafing dish as did some scrambled eggs. Honey-Lemon muffins with peach butter sat nestled in a napkin-covered basket and sausages, bacon and freshly sliced ham completed out the menu.

Tiara felt her mouth-watering as she poured herself a cup of black coffee and grabbed a slice of bacon and began munching away.

She was on her second cup of coffee when the door opened, and Delmar strolled in, with a briefcase in hand.

"Where're my clothes?" She asked taking a sip of coffee before she noticed the briefcase. "What is in the briefcase?" She asked as she munched on a piece of ham.

"Well, I had your dress sent down to be cleaned," he said. "I see you found the clothes I had the hotel concierge pick out for you? Do you like them?"

"Yes, I do and by the way, thank you."

Tiara stared into the cup of coffee she was enjoying and smiled. She'd forgotten how generous Delmar could be when he wanted to. Or wanted something. Her thoughts overtook her as she took another sip of coffee and thought back to the night before. She wondered about the last drink Delmar had gotten for her. The blue cocktail that made everything feel like heaven. She remembered back to when Delmar wanted her best friend Camille Baptiste-Garcia. He wanted her so badly that he'd put something in her drink as well. She put down her coffee. It left a bad taste in her mouth.

She closed her eyes and said a quiet prayer and then said. "What are you playing at Delmar? Don't forget I know what you are capable of!"

Delmar sat down at the table and fixed himself a plate of scrambled eggs and ham. "You and I got history together, Tiara," he hesitated. "Not to mention two beautiful sons, who deserve stability in their lives."

Instantly, Tiara rose. "If you think for one minute, I'm going to let you take my boys away from me…"

"Sit down, Tiara and finish eating your food. And stop looking at me like I put something in your coffee. I don't do that sort of thing anymore. Those days, of my doing stupid nonsense like that are over. Besides our past is behind us. I know I've lied to you many times, and you lied to me many times. But when it is all said and done your heart belongs to me."

Tiara couldn't believe this was Delmar she was sitting there talking too. He was a completely changed man, she thought as she slowly paced the floor and stared back at him.

Delmar poured himself a cup of coffee and took a big gulp and then picked up a fork full of scrambled eggs and began eating.

His movements comforted Tiara, she guessed he wouldn't drink the coffee if he had put something in it, so she sat back down and filled her plate with some scrambled eggs and started eating.

All at once Delmar leaned over to her and put his hand on top of hers. He gave her a steady look. "I have to be honest with you and admit that I made a mistake."

It was precisely at that moment Delmar spoke that Tiara felt like something cold brush up against her leg. She peered down. There was nothing there.

"Did you hear me Tiara?"Delmar inquired.

"You mean about not acknowledging your sons, or how you treated me?" Tiara asked in disbelief, shaking out her thoughts. She felt like something was in the room with them or was it her mind playing tricks on her?

Delmar nodded. "Look, I cannot explain my behavior or why I did what I did. Nor can I excuse what I did. All I know is that I'm truly sorry for the way I've treated you and my sons," he replied, as a yearning of disbelief washed over him.

Listening intently she turned her full attention to him. "Why, Delmar, I've never seen this side of you before," she murmured, feeling joy deep within believing that he had finally changed.

Delmar's eyes glazed over as he stared out transfixed. "You were so young and beautiful," he muttered, lost at the moment, spellbound and not comprehending what he was speaking. "But your people were just very poor. Dirt poor. They should have furnished better for your dowry."

Startled Tiara could have sworn Delmar's voice changed. She saw his lips move, but the speech was distinctly different. "Dowry? What dowry are you talking about, Delmar?" She asked but didn't wait for his response. "What's wrong with you Delmar?"

"You're no good," he moaned again, as if in a trance.

"You are acting strange Delmar. Like you're another person?"

A frisson passed over him. He felt strange. "I know, I'm not me... I mean I don't know. I'm not myself."

Tiara cocked her head. "Are you drunk? Do you have a hangover from last night?"

"No... No... I'm not drunk. Maybe intoxicated. But I'm not drunk," he snarled and then started his rant again. "You were so caring... I can't believe you would kill your own child... You... You, bitch!"

She blinked back tears. "Fuck you! You son of a bitch! How dare you talk to me like that! I never killed my child!" She yelled instantly rising and putting some distance between them.

"What? What's wrong?" Delmar asked, his eyes still filmy and glazed over.

Before he could figure out what was happening Tiara walked over and slapped him hard across the face.

"Ouch! What was that for?" He yelled waking out of his trance.

"Look, Delmar I don't know what kind of sick game you are playing at, but I've never killed any baby. Mine or anybody's else," she blurted, turning to make her exit.

"Tiara! Wait a minute. Why did you slap me?"

"I never killed any baby!"

Delmar closed the gap between them. "I don't remember saying anything about your killing a baby. All I remember is that you slapped me. It was like... Like you woke me up. Like I was sleepwalking or something."

"What are you playing at Delmar? What kind of game is this?"

He shook his head. "I don't know what's going on. Everything feels so weird. I wanted to talk to you. I thought everything was going to be perfect. All I had to do was tell you that I made a mistake that we should together, show you the prenuptial agreement and get you to sign…"

Tiara shook her head. "Prenup? Sign? Delmar, what are you talking about?"

He howled out a snicker and then the insults floated off his tongue. "Whore! Slut! You bedswerver! Trollop! Sign the fucking Prenup!"

"Screw you, Delmar!" Tiara yelled, astonished at the crazy way Delmar was carrying on. It was like the man was possessed.

Delmar hesitated for a second and tried to shake out his thoughts. Things weren't going as he'd planned. Words were coming out of his mouth that he wasn't putting there. Tiara wasn't understanding him. Something strange was happening.

"Jesus Christ!" Delmar blurted out loud, slapping his head. He moaned in agony and started muttering succinctly. "I'm not a praying man, but I think I'm under a spell or something… I can't even control what I'm saying."

Tiara took a step back from him. "I don't know what the hell is wrong with you, Delmar! But you're making me scared. I'm getting the hell out of here!"

"No! No! Wait, Tiara! It's not me… I swear it! It's… It's…," he tried to explain, but the words died on his tongue. All at once he began blurting controllably. "You're a fool! You're a fool! You stupid bitch!"

"Oh, yeah!" Tiara yelled, heading for the door. "Well I've got news for you Delmar you're a crazy bastard!"

Before he could stop her, Tiara opened the door and rushed out of it. She ran like the devil was chasing her. She didn't even have to press the elevator button. The door just opened for her as if by magic.

Chapter 9

Tiara, Diademe, & Camille

Tiara sat hidden in a back corner of the coffee shop on the first floor of the Fairmont hotel. She was grateful to the front desk for letting her call her best friend Camille to come and pick her up.

Her thoughts traveled back to what had happened between her and Delmar and she marveled how he went from acting like he had good sense, to acting like a crazy person in less than ten minutes.

A familiar strange floral scent consumed the air. Tiara looked around wondering where it was coming from.

She was gawking off into space when a beam of light flashed in the corner of her eye caught her attention just as a cold breeze of air surrounded her and made her shiver.

"Good morning Dearie are you cold? Might I suggest you join me in a cup of hot tea or coffee? It will warm you up."

"Hello … Oh, no," Tiara said, before returning the gaze of the woman.

Tiara was silently taken back, when she held the woman's gaze for a long moment. A slight, crooked smile sat on the mouth of a most beautiful woman, who didn't look like anything of this world.

Even the woman's clothes seemed old and ancient, yet stylish and beautiful. She watched as the woman wrapped a beautifully embroidered sapphire pashmina shawl closely around her.

"I hope I didn't frighten you," the woman said, "My name is Diademe. Won't you please join me in a hot beverage, my treat. I hate drinking alone."

"Thank you; Diademe, my name is Tiara and I'd love a cup of coffee, black, if you don't mind, please."

Tiara waited while Diademe got the attention of a waitress and ordered their drinks. She watched while Diademe chitchatted with their waitress, with her old-fashioned charming manners, it gave her time to let her mind wander. Her thoughts kept going back to Delmar and his crazy talk. She just couldn't seem to wrap her mind around what had happened.

"I don't suppose you've ever given much thought to a love potion," Diademe mentioned. "You'd be astonished at how it can do wonders for a bad relationship. Are you engaged to be married to your young man? A love potion will help get him down the matrimony aisle."

"I beg your pardon," Tiara snapped out of her thoughts. She was sure she hadn't heard her correctly. "Are you for real? You're talking about a love potion?"

"As it so happens, I am," Diademe responded, a little breathless. "A love spell can help even the worst relationship overcome a hurdle or two. Of course, you'd have to use a strong love spell for those cases, cause the object is to make the man know that you are alive, among the living," she replied taking a deep breath.

The waitress brought over their drinks and sat them on the table. She nodded at Diademe before walking away.

Tiara notice, Diademe had difficulty breathing, also as if she wasn't used to breathing the smog filled air of San Jose. "Your tea smells wonderful. Perhaps you should have a sip of your tea, it may help your throat," she suggested.

Diademe cleared her throat. "Later, my new friend. I am waiting for it to cool. You're welcome to a cup if you like. I ordered enough for two."

"Thank you, but I'd like to finish my coffee first," Tiara said picking up her cup of black coffee and taking a sip before going back to their topic of conversation. "I've never taken much interest in a love potion, that stuff is just mumbo-jumbo. If a man loves you, he loves you for you, period."

"You sound bitter, perhaps the man I saw you dancing with you last night has made you feel that way. If you don't mind my saying so, he isn't worthy of you, especially if he hasn't yet proposed."

"You saw me dancing with Delmar? You were at the fundraiser last night?"

"Oh, yes. I enjoyed attending," Diademe blinked drowsily at Tiara, her eyes full of torment and sorrow. "So, are you in love with this fellow named, Delmar? Has he proposed to you?"

"I… I." Tiara took a quick breath. "You keep asking me if he's proposed. It's kind of complicated. We have children together. So, yes, I guess I do kind of… Maybe love him."

"Children, what are they? Boys or girls?"

Tiara's face beamed with pride. "Their twin boys."

Diademe smiled softly. "Sent by an angel from above, I'm sure. I can tell that you love them."

"Yes, I do. I love them very much," Tiara said. "They make me glad that I'm alive."

Diademe nodded and said with a lackluster wave. "Without love, there is no reason to live."

Tiara studied Diademe. She was unique looking, like she was not of this world.

All at once Diademe waved her hand as if dismissing the whole subject. In a voice that was sleepy, calmly she said, "By the way, getting back to Delmar, I don't trust him, there was something about him that seemed sinister, like he's hiding a secret from you Tiara, take my word for it. If he hasn't proposed to you, he is hiding something."

Such a strange voice, so preternaturally wise, all-knowing, sweet, and calm, Tiara thought, as she peered back at Diademe. She blinked back at her until she thought like she was starting to appear… unsettled. A strange churning feeling was bubbling in the pit of her stomach. "Propose? Why? I mean ..."

Tiara couldn't even finish her sentence before a jumble of images flashed before her eyes. A full bright moon flashed and seared across her field of vision. A baby appeared, not her own. Who's was it? Her heart pounded. Suddenly a man's stern looking face appeared and then fire flamed in his dark blank eyes, and then a shovel was thrust into a grave and the dirt was flung, as she felt pain. Terror, pain, and anguish made her feel sick. Instantaneously, she woke from her daydream with a startling gasp.

"Tiara? Are you alright?"

Tiara gasped and grasped her arms tightly around her. She felt disoriented. Slowly she nodded and took a deep breath and remembered where she was. She said the first thing that popped into her head. "Why would you say something like that? I mean about

Delmar proposing?"

Diademe blinked drowsily and answered. "Why not?" She shrugged. "If a man can pass through paradise in a dream and the dwarf becomes a giant, one world is no different from another," she replied shaking her head. "And the dreamer can be anyone he chooses."

The churning in the pit of Tiara's stomach coupled with a splitting headache she was suffering had her feeling bewildered and overwhelmed. "Excuse me, but Diademe, that just doesn't make sense to me."

"And neither does life, to the living," Diademe added, leaning over and patting Tiara's hand.

"Tiara Blake! I've been looking all over this hotel for you," Camille shrilled cry carried on the air as she crossed the room.

Tiara lifted out of her seat and took a couple steps forward as Camille closed the distance between them.

"Camille, it's so good to see you," Tiara said, hugging her friend and talking a mile a minute. "Girlfriend, have I got so much to tell. I've been having a conversation with a very interesting woman, while I was waiting for you. I can't tell you how much her sitting with me, while I waited for you, has comforted me."

Camille took a good look at Tiara from head to toe and knew she had had a life-changing experience. She wished she had invited Eris Simeon to come with her. The three of them were old friends. Whenever anyone of them was going through a personal crisis, they each would be there to give her support.

All at once Tiara stopped. "I'm sorry Camille I haven't introduced you to Diademe," she said turning around to face her table, before stopping abruptly.

The smile died on Tiara's face. She glanced around the restaurant. A tiny frown marred her brow, as she shook her head. She lifted her gaze and looked at Camille. "That's strange, Diademe was sitting here just a minute ago. I don't know where she could have gone too, that fast."

Camille noticed how nervous Tiara was acting. "Tiara let's sit down, you can tell me what happened and start from the beginning," she paused. "It looks like you order enough tea for two people and there are fresh cups and saucers."

Tiara's dark eyes widen bewildered, as she looked around nervously. Her voice shook when she spoke. "That's just it. I didn't order the tea or the coffee. Like I told you it was Diademe. She..."

A familiar strange floral scent engulfed the air just as a chill breeze swept past them.

The atmosphere felt surreal.

Tiara shivered. "It's cold, I want to leave."

Camille felt the change in the atmosphere at the same time Tiara did. "Come on then, let's go home," she said, taking her hand.

Chapter 10

I was confused!

"Are you joking me? You meet up with Delmar Devereaux at the Annual Music Heart Gala, and you slept with him?" Eris Simeon exclaimed. "Talk about some sick, twisted bullshit!"

Camille gave Eris a disparaging glance. "Life can have many forks in the road. Sometimes shit just happens. It's ain't Tiara's fault if her body was weak."

Eris blurted. "Weak my ass! She was fucking horny."

"Eris and Camille! Stop cursing the twins are sleeping in the next room," Tiara cautioned.

"Okay, we are sorry for that little four-letter French word, but you do know Tiara that Camille and I are both thinking the same thing."

"What?" Tiara inquired.

"That he put something in your drink," Camille and Eris replied in unison.

"No disrespect, Tiara, but you do recall what Delmar is capable of?" She suggested but didn't wait for a response. "Remember what he did to me and Desmond? He drugged us," Camille stated.

"Come on Camille, I know you are thinking what I'm thinking," Eris expressed. "Not to mention he probably put something in her drink."

"I know all of that I was there, I remember. It's just that I was confused. I don't know what I was thinking. I know I had no business sleeping with Delmar," she replied as her thoughts raced. *"But, part of me keep remembering how good his penis felt..."*

Tiara took a deep sigh and spoke out loud. "The next thing I knew, I was suddenly jumping into bed with him... And then..."

"You had sex! I knew it! From the look on your face, I can tell you enjoyed it, extremely so, Tiara!" Eris laughed out hysterically.

"I did not," Tiara lied, and suddenly responded in her

defense. "It was his flattery that succeeded in getting me to yield to the wiles of that man."

Camille smirked knowingly. "Yeah, the wiles of a man laying down some *excellent pipe*! It will get you every time and have you falling under his spell," she laughed.

Eris expressed a modest snicker. "Yeah, but what kept Tiara riding his tricky dick ass, all night? Oh, yeah, it must have been that sweet talk and flattery words, and not his pumping you hard with his hard piece of wood," she laughed.

"Camille and Eris," Tiara replied, flipping the two of them a salty look. "You two are just mean-spirited and evil. You are so lucky I love you both like my sisters. Otherwise, I'd be kicking your asses, right about now."

Camillie and Eris shook with laughter.They yelled in unisom. "Yeah, right!"

All at once Tiara smiled wide and threw up her hands and started laughing. "You know, when I stop and think about it, there was some really crazy shit, happening that night!"

"Well, I need to get out of here, Ladies, I do have a man to go home too and Desmond detests having to eat his dinner alone," Camille answered.

Tiara began clearing away her dining room table and the stopped abruptly and looked up. "Oh, yeah, Camille about that exercise class you told me about. I signed up for it and I reviewed the references on Linda Perrin, Odessa Johnson's granddaughter and she checks out as a superb babysitter."

"See I told you," Camille replied. "Even Eris admires her. She couldn't find any fault with her."

"And you know I tried," Eris interrupted. "If I hadn't signed up for the exercise class myself, I'd stay home and watch my little Godson, myself."

Snatching up her handbag, Camille headed for the front door. "Come on Eris, you rode with me, remember?"

"Okay… Okay!" Eris added, following Camille outside of the car.

Tiara watched calmly from her front door as her two friends got into Camille's Lexus and drove away.

For the next few minutes, Tiara busied herself tidying up

behind her friends and enjoying the quiet while the twins were still asleep.

The phone rang, and she rolled her eyes and grasped it on the first ring. "Hello?" She whispered.

A familiar male voice blared through the phone. "Hi, gorgeous did you enjoy yourself the other night at the Annual Music Heart Gala?"

"Zack? Why?" She anxiously asked and suddenly added. "I mean, I didn't see you, where you there?"

"No, sorry baby, I wasn't," he replied. "Isla Wickham said she saw you there."

Tiara breathed out a sigh of relief. She knew Isla hadn't filled Zack in on Delmar, otherwise, it would have been the first thing out of his mouth.

Zack went on. "Don't you know if I had been there I would have asked you to dance? I heard you looked so beautiful in your red evening dress. I sure hate I missed seeing you in that. In fact, I was calling to see if you wanted to go out with me?"

Tiara drew in a heavy breath about to express something. "I... Ahhhh..."

"I know that you interviewed Odessa's granddaughter to be a babysitter for you and the girl is free tonight."

Strange that at the mention of Odessa's name. She knew exactly what had happened. "Let me guess," Tiara replied. "Odessa told you?"

"Yes, you know I see her at the hospital all the time and Odessa tells everybody's business," Zack said.

Tiara let out a dull snort. "Yes, don't I know it. Thank God Linda is nothing like her grandmother."

He inhaled a breath. "Anyway, you'll like what I've got planned for tonight, and we can make an evening of it. Please don't say no."

"Oh, alright. I'll go out with you tonight, but first I have to call Linda and see if she's available," Tiara replied.

"No, worries, I already have," Zack explained. "I even asked Linda if she needed a ride, but she said she'll drive herself over if you needed her."

"Well it looks like you have everything already arranged, I'll just wait for you to pick me up," she declared.

***

Hours later that same night, Tiara was cruising down Highway 101 feeling on top of the world. When Zack had asked if she didn't mind meeting him at the nightclub tonight. She'd jumped at the opportunity to drive herself. It afforded her a rare chance to drive her jet-black Corvette; it was the one thing from her days of being single and carefree that she'd kept. Since having the twins, she rarely got to drive her Corvette. She gave up driving her little sports car daily because she needed the space in her Chevy mini-van for carting the twins, their car seats, stroller and all the other equipment she seemed to need to handle raising them.

The Matilda exit signaling she reached the town of Sunnyvale, loomed in front of her as she hastily made the exit.

A few minutes later she pulled to the curb on Murphy street in front of the building that was built to resemble an old Southern house complete with a humongous wraparound porch.

The house was the epitome of the Garden District in New Orleans complete with "Southern Charm". The many verandas and porches made the look complete. Locals said the Southern Charm made it the perfect place to enjoy making new friends or catching up with old friends while enjoying a glass of Southern Sweet Tea if your taste buds desired or a stronger tea such as the Long Island variety. The old southern charm on the outside of the home was a cover for the nightclub to be found inside.

Tiara stretched her long lean legs as she got out of her corvette and walked up to the house.   Several couples were sitting on the porch talking and laughing as the beat of sweet soft jazz music filled the air.

Tiara started to walk toward the front door when she paused. She thought she smelled a familiar mystic fragrance.

Instantly Zack showed up out of nowhere. "I think you'll

going to love this place. They have dance music inside."

"I think I will too," Tiara agreed, as Zack rested his hand on the small of her back and lead her inside.

The place was crowded inside with a lively and friendly atmosphere. Zack seemed to be a regular here and knew exactly where to go. He led then deep inside into a room with a huge dance floor.

A hostess greeted them, and Zack whispered something into her ear. She then took them to a table overlooking the dance floor.

"This spot is excellent," Tiara said. "We only have to step down to the dance floor."

"Would you like to order your drinks now," their waitress asked.

"Yes," Tiara blurted. "I'll take a fruity drink, what do you recommend?"

"Our mango margarita is a house specialty," the hostess stated.

"Excellent, I'll have that," Tiara said.

"And I'll have a beer," Zack said. "Make it a Bud in the bottle."

Zack turned his attention to Tiara. "Would you like something to eat? Before we start dancing?"

"Sure, I heard the Cajun Appetizer Platter was famous here," Tiara said. "I've never tried it. They say the Cajun Fried Calamari is excellent. What do you think?"

"I think great minds think alike," Zack smiled.

A few minutes later their waitress brought over their drinks and the Cajun Appetizer Platter.

Tiara took a sip of her mango margarita. "Wow, this is tasty. Momma likes a lot," she declared before grabbing a cornmeal battered Fried Shrimp and closing her eyes as she savored the first bite.

"It's good, huh?" Zack asked as he shoved a sausage ball into his mouth. "I had these before, they are the best I know of on the west coast."

For the next twenty minutes, Tiara and Zack chitchatted and

caught up on old times as they feasted on the deep-fried cornmeal battered shrimp, fried crab meatballs, sausage balls, and Cajun fried Calamari.

Tiara let out a heavy groan. "I'm so full, I can't eat another bite."

"How about we go hit the dance floor?" Zack suggested.

Once on the dance floor, Tiara stood fascinated as Zack began moving his body back and forth to the sound of the beat.

Tiara laughed. "Uh! I see you've got moves.".

Almost instantly she detected a familiar strange floral scent engulfed in the air.

She glanced around wondering where it was coming from, across the dance floor she thought she saw, Diademe, just as Zack wrapped his arms around her laughing, as he did, and twirl her mindlessly in circles.

When she finally composed herself and looked back to the spot where she thought she saw Diademe, she was gone.

"I think that mango margarita was a lot stronger than it looked, she thought to herself as she kept dancing.

The next thing she knew the DJ started playing some upbeat dance tune and the next thing Tiara knew she and Zack were lost spellbound in the music moving about the dance floor.

Chapter 11

THE JOURNEY AND NONA & DELMAR

One thing was certain Delmar knew he needed help. His ego had gotten in the way early when he thought he could take matters into his own hands and persuade Tiara to marry him. Now he knew drastic times called for drastic measures and the only way to break the curse was to follow Nona, Glenda and Consuela's solution. The quest to find the items to break the curse was the only way.

Going back to Nona, Glenda, and Consuela hadn't been easy for him. But when he realized he couldn't handle the matter all by himself, he knew he needed help and he knew the three ladies were the only ones who could help him.

Delmar couldn't believe he had agreed to go on this journey, he looked around the rooftop of the San Mateo History Museum. The old museum was a historic monument and was the pride of joy of Redwood City. The domed stained-glass was thought to be the largest of its kind on the West Coast and was known by many to have important significance to some unknown power.

He surveyed the domed stained-glass for another minute and then shrugged his shoulders and turned his attention to Nona. She stood silently in the background watchful.

Nona knew the minute she looked at the huge stained-glass dome ceiling, why the first clue was to be obtained at the San Mateo History Museum in Redwood City because just the size alone made the dome ceiling a superb portal for traveling through time. She concentrated her mind on something she studied about the stained-glass dome and how it related to, portal travel.

Nona glance at the full moon making its way across the sky. She nodded with understanding, the moon was also a transporting portal opening the gates to other realms.

Delmar loudly cleared his throat. "What are we waiting for again Nona?"

Nona looked at him with a bewildered expression. "It's she, and her name is Mistress Pleasant."

Delmar leaned back and squeezed his fingers to his temple. He recognized he wasn't psychic. But since he'd been hanging around Nona, Glenda and Consuela he'd started to perceive things. He could feel something was about to happen.

Lightning flashed as storm clouds raged.

At the first burst of lighting, Delmar closed his eyes when he opened them. A nut-brown woman descended out of a small floating galaxy of stars, fog, and clouds.

"I smell a descendant of Marie Laveau," the nut-brown woman spoke, as she drifted in closer. "I am called Mistress Pleasant and you are?" She asked gliding her path over to Nona.

"Greetings Mistress Pleasant. I am Nona Laveau and I am the descendant of Marie Laveau," she waved her hand. "And this is Delmar Deveraux."

"Ahhhh and so he is!" Mistress Pleasant exclaimed. "It's uncanny he looks just like that old devil he descended from."

Delmar looked like he didn't understand. But thought better of saying anything.

Nona looked perplexed. "Old devil?"

Mistress Pleasant nodded. "His relative," she answered, waving her hand at Delmar, "The one who he is here representing," she shook her head. "But who has time to explain physics of the soul? Rest assured Delmar and his relative are one and the same. Now let's stop all this talk. We haven't much time, the bewitching hour is near."

Delmar found his voice and asked. "The bewitching hour? What is that?"

Nona looked at Delmar. "It is the time of night when the veil between our world and the domain of the supernatural is pulled aside."

"Which makes it the best time to travel by portal. We'll make good time," Mistress Pleasant said. "We must go to the heart of the gold country to see the magic mermaid of Moaning Caverns."

Delmar nervously cleared his throat. "Magic mermaid? I never heard of such a thing and I have been to the Moaning Caverns many times."

Nona returned to the moment and recognized she needed to rein Delmar in. "Look Delmar you are not dealing with what you see in the natural world, right now. Just be open to having a new adventure."

"Delmar, my son," Mistress Pleasant said. "Might I suggest to you to drop by a friendly little bookstore in Berkley called Ye Olde Book Shoppe, you will find it on the corner of Shattuck and Vine Street. Ask for Pegasus and tell him you are looking for the book "How To Never Get Lost In Time" by Hermione Potter," it's an excellent book and been around for centuries."

"Now let me see if I got that straight," Delmar said querulously. "I'm to go to Ye old Book Shoppe, in Berkley, and see a guy named Pegasus and ask him for a book called "How To Never Get Lost In Time" by Hermione Potter. Wow, that does sound tempting? I'll be an expert on time travel in no time."

Nona heard Delmar's sarcasm and turned to Mistress Pleasant. "Don't worry about Delmar getting an understanding of anything, stupidly is as stupid does, just get this journey started." "Good!" Mistress Pleasant said. "I don't have time to give Delmar any fairy food so that he can fly. Besides, we need to get out of here before we wake the troll who haunts the Superior Court building across the street. I amazed that nosey troll hasn't snuck up on us already. Now, Delmar take my hand and don't let go until we reach our destination."

Chapter 12

Lady Eidothea

"I never wish to set foot in another caven for as long as I live," Delmar thought to himself as the three travelers descended deeper and further below the surface of the earth.

When they first started down into the cavern, he'd thought the landscape induces an illusion of benevolence, it was the most beautiful place he'd ever seen as the variety of white, cream and caramel colored crystalline walls glistened in front of him.

Now one thing was certain, he knew that the level Mistress Pleasant had brought them two would never be seen by common everyday tourist, because the underworld landscape here was unique, surreal, and hidden so far beneath the earth's surface no sane person would want to travel there.

He noticed pools of water coming into view until finally, Mistress Pleasant bought them to a standstill in front of a huge glowing lake.

At first, Delmar thought that it was just a large fishtail laying on the bank of the lake nestled by a large helictite rock. But as they drew closer, more details came into view.

Graceful arms were attached to a slim waist that clung to a greenish blue-gray fish scales.

Delmar knew the sound that came out of his mouth didn't sound like him. "Do… Do… Do you see her?" He exclaimed. "It… It's a real mermaid!"

"Shhhhh!" Nona cautioned.

The mermaid had sharp ears. Her voice was dry and whispery. "Who approaches me?"

Mistress Pleasant moved in closer to the mermaid. "Lady Eidothea, it is I, Mistress Pleasant, I come with friends."

"Bring them closer so that I can see them," Lady Eidothea commanded.

Mistress Pleasant waved her hand at Nona. "This is Nona…"

Lady Eidothea interrupted. "You bring a descendant of Marie Laveau, I can tell her bond is strong," she wavered. "And who is the gentleman?"

"This is Delmar Devereaux," Mistress Pleasant stated.

"So, you want us to have a conversation about ethics in magic?" Lady Eidothea laughed. "Please Mistress Pleasant, spare me. Desperate people do daring things. This is the commodity and exchange game. I've got something Delmar needs to break a curse and I need something from him. That is the deal, take it or leave it."

Mistress Pleasant exhaled and shook her head. Finally, she spoke. "Very well, if it is the only way, we can have what we need when you leave me no choice. Delmar!" She yelled.

Delmar stepped forward at the commanding sound of her voice. "Yes Mistress," he promptly said.

"Hold on wait a minute," Mistress Pleasant said, turning her attention. "Lady Eidothea your request... I mean what commodity would you like to exchange for giving us what we have need of?"

Lady Eidothea cleared her throat. "I require Delmar to escort me to the Black and White Masquerade Ball, in San Francisco, on December 31."

Delmar's lips curled into disgust. He couldn't believe what he just heard Lady Eidothea say. His reaction was a natural response as he exclaimed out with mirth. "You can't be serious!" He snickered. "Sorry, but do you understand you're not human? You have no legs to walk into the Masquerade Ball, and I seriously think is illegal to cart you there in a giant fishbowl, if we could even find one."

He turned chuckling.

Behind him, he heard the footsteps smashing against small pebble stones. He knew it was Nona. She gently tapped his shoulder as she peered at Lady Eidothea. "Delmar, stop laughing," she whispered. "Don't be a fool. Think of what you are doing here."

"I can't help it," he whispered through clenched teeth. "You bought me on this quest and now you expect me to take a fish to a New Year's Eve Ball. In fact, the biggest New Year's Eve Ball on the West Coast. I can't do that. Besides, I'm planning on being married by New Year's Eve and what do you think my wife will do when I say, *Oh, by the way, honey, I've got to take a Mermaid to the New Year's Ball instead of you?*"

Mistress Pleasant glided over "Delmar you are a pompous and headstrong as they come. Women are simple creatures but human or not, they all suffer the pain of mean-spirited words," she replied, glaring back toward Lady Eidothea.

Delmar followed her glanced. The sad and melancholy expression on Lady Eidothea's face struck a chord in his heart. Since he began hanging around Glenda, Nona, and Consuela and their pack of ever-increasing female friends he'd found his feeling had become more in tuned to how he related to women.

Mistress Pleasant continued talking. "Your words can do them damage, Delmar. Even if it wasn't intended. Do you not realize the power of your words? How they can hurt?"

Delmar's thoughts got the best of him. Visions of Tiara's face flashed before him. It reminded him of the sad expression on Tiara's face when he'd won his case against her in court. Then like now, Delmar had allowed his ego and pride to run amok and humiliate a woman just for the power feeling it gave.

"I see your mind is churning Delmar," Mistress Pleasant said, whispering in his ear. "You realize the error of your ways by hurting someone just because you believe you have the power to do so. It is truly because you've never had a thought for anyone's else's feelings, but your own."

Delmar knew the point she was making had taken hold when he felt a deep sadness clinging to the silence of the moment. He swallowed hard as he watched tears slid gently down Lady Eidothea's face before she closed her deep green eyes and let her half fish body slid down curving around the stone as she slid into the dark lake water. In seconds she was immersed completely. A single bubble of air wafted to the surface of the lake and then it disappeared.

The silence was excruciating. Delmar swallowed hard, his mouth dry and pained his throat, as he stared back at the calmness of the lake water where Lady Eidothea had gone in.

The current of the lake pushed against the rocks and made an eerie splash. Delmar felt his heart pounding. *What have I done?* He thought to himself. *What have I done?*

After what seemed like forever, he had a fierce revelation that he had to make things right. He found his voice and yelled. "Lady Eidothea! Lady Eidothea! Are you there?" he pleaded and prayed. "Please forgive me for making fun of you. I am so sorry! I will escort you any place that you like. Please come back!"

The lake water was still and calm as Delmar stared back. His breath left his body as he thought about what he had done, leaving his speechless as he looked back at the water.

In the silence of the moment, Delmar almost jumped out of his skin when he heard footsteps near him. "I'm so sorry Delmar," Nona softly replied. "It looks like Lady Eidothea has gone. We should leave now."

The current of the rocks pushed back and forth, growing harder with every second. Instantly a fierce loud splash of water sent a drenching mist their way as Lady Eidothea swam over.

"So, Delmar, did you mean what you said?" Lady Eidothea asked as she drew closer. "You will escort me?"

"Yes... Yes!" He exclaimed. "I'm so sorry if I offended you."

Lady Eidothea flipped her tail. "By the way Delmar, for your information I will have legs on the night of December 31. I am allowed land legs that night," she said settling her gaze on the three sets of eyes in front of her.

Delmar looked pleased. "Wow, now that will make me very happy."

Nona saw her need to take charge. "Lady Eidothea since Delmar, agreed, can we get on with why we are here?"

"Yes, but first I want to hear a complete sentence on what Delmar has promised me. It is part of the bargain," Lady Eidothea replied.

Puzzled Delmar stuttered. "But... But!"

"Agreed!" Nona commanded, gritted teeth. "Say it, Delmar."

"Ok, very well, if I must. I agree to take Lady Eidothea to the Black and White Masquerade Ball on December 31!"

"Thank goodness," Mistress Pleasant smiled.

Frantic Delmar blurted "Even though I'm telling you right now, I'm not coming down to this cavern to pick you up, Sister you'd better find a way to meet me in San Jose!"

"Don't worry Delmar, I'll meet you in San Jose," Lady Eidothea said.

Nona patted Delmar on the back. "We're almost done here."

Lady Eidothea took a deep breath. "Now Nona, come and take what you must, I'm ready," she commanded.

Nona walked over and stumped down on one knee, she placed her hand gently under a large fish scale on Lady Eidothea body and said. "I hope this doesn't hurt too much," she said pulling forcibly.

She placed the scale securely in a velvet bag and hid it in the cloak she wore.

"I Thank You Lady Eidothea as do Delmar too," Nona said. "Now what is our next clue?"

"In three days' time, you must go and see the White Witch of the Auburn mines," Lady Eidothea said.

"Why in three days? Why can't we go now?" Delmar asked.

"Because it will be daylight soon," Mistress Pleasant stated. "And you need to get some rest, Delmar."

Puzzled Delmar blurted. "But how will we know what to ask the White Witch for?"

"You need a lock of her hair," Lady Eidothea said with a serious look on her face. She looked back at the strained look on Delmar's face and then laughed. "It was a joke! You can't get a lock of hair from a ghost."

Nona blurted out a laugh and shook her head. "That was funny."

Delmar gave an ironic smile. "A mermaid with jokes, what is the world coming too?"

"Seriously," Lady Eidothea said. "The White Witch will tell you what you need next and where to go to get it. And remember Nona, only a descendant of Marie Laveau may touch the item or the curse cannot be broken."

"Yes, I understand," Nona replied. "Now I'll take Delmar home."

"Look ladies I don't mind being lead around at night, in the dark by three beautiful ladies, but a man doesn't live by beautifying alone," he explained as his stomach rumbled loudly.

"The empty beast of a man, known as his stomach growls in hungry," Mistress Pleasant chuckled. "The sons of Adam never changes."

"The man is famished, please feed him," Lady Eidothea stated as she slid back down into the lake waters.

Nona laughed. "Some things never change, come on Delmar take my hand let me get you back to civilization and a twenty-four-hour coffee shop as quick as possible."

Chapter 13
Coincidence, Coffee & You

The twenty-four-hour coffee shop looked warm, comfortable, and inviting, Tiara reflected as she navigated her car into a parking space. She was glad that Zack had called up her at the last minute and had her drive her car and meet her at the late nightclub on Murphy Avenue in Sunnyvale.

Dancing the night away had been entertaining at four o'clock in the morning on the huge dance floor at Pure Ice Nightclub. Zack had the night off, but his on-call status at the emergency room meant he'd be the first in line when an emergency came up. They had made it just ten-mutes past the four o'clock a.m. hour before he received the call.

Tiara couldn't understand why she'd left the club without using the ladies room and she couldn't believe her stomach was growling so loudly. That was when she concluded the twenty-four-hour coffee shop was the place she needed to be.

A familiar strange floral scent engulfed the air. Tiara looked around wondering where it was coming from. the smell reminded her of *Diademe; she reflected* as the name rolled off her tongue.

She wandered inside and promptly asked the hostess. "Where is the bathroom?"

"Down the hallway to your left," she said, pointing her finger in the direction Tiara should go.

Tiara easily discovered the ladies room and was glad that there wasn't a line. She did her business, washed her hands and proceeded to put on a fresh coat of lipstick out of habit, just before she came out and went looking for the hostess to find her a seat.

"Tiara? What are you doing here?"

At the sound of Delmar's voice, Tiara stopped dead in her tracks and swung around and gawked at him.

"Hi, Delmar? I could ask you the same thing," she exhaled, turning to get a good look at him. *"Damn, "* he looked so good she thought.

Loudly she cleared her throat. "I was just going to look for the hostess and have her find me a seat."

"You don't have too," he added. "I mean you are welcome to join me. I'm dining alone, same as you."

Tiara didn't know why her feet betrayed her as she wandered over to him. *"Damn, he smells so good, "* she thought to herself as she brushed past him and took the seat across from him. "Thanks, for inviting me to sit down. I'm really hungry."

"I'm glad you could join me," he grinned. "The breakfast here is really good."

Tiara looked at his plate. "Yes, you're having the Country Big Breakfast. I could do with the junior portion myself and some black coffee."

Delmar got the attention of their waiter and place her order. Before finally turning to get a good look at her. "You look like you had a night of dancing."

Tiara felt her face warming up. Anxiety was all over her face. "How did you know that?"

"You're wearing that black Latin swing dress you always loved to go dancing in," he beamed. "You always look marvelous in it when you are twirling and spinning around the dance floor."

She laughed and looked down at her dress. "You remembered about me and my favorite dress. I'm touched," she breathed. "Sounds like there's hope for you yet."

"Damn, Delmar looked good," she thought.

The waiter brought her food.

Tiara took a big fork full of eggs and country potatoes. "You would think I haven't eaten," she said swallowing. "Just hours ago, I was feasting on fried shrimp, calamari, and crab balls."

"I think you must have worked it off, with all of your dancing," Delmar said.

"I think you're right," she replied, chewing a sausage.

Delmar offered her a smile. "Can I ask what happened to your date?"

"What do you mean?" she asked and then continued before he could reply. "Oh, you mean where's he's at. Well, we're not really a boyfriend and girlfriend item. Not like you and I were. You know with that combust love thing we got. If you know what I mean?"

Silence. The kind the comes after a bomb has been dropped.

She shrugged. She wished she hadn't spoken her mind, especially when she realized memories of her passionate last night with Delmar was wrecking havoc on her senses. "Ignore me. I don't know why I said that."

His eyes roamed all over her face searching. She wasn't like other women. With other women, he'd been with they had never cared about him. Just his money and what he could do for them. Tiara was different, after all, he'd put her through he knew her heart was with him. She deserved more from him then she could ever imagine. He could handle giving her more. "I can't ignore it. I keep seeing images of you and me that last night we were together. You know when everything was just so perfect."

Tiara laughed but didn't say anything thinking back to when she thought she saw Diademe across the dance floor. What was it she had said about a love potion? She shook out her thoughts and said. "It seems like minds think alike, I've been thinking about the last night we were together, also. Tell me, Delmar, I don't suppose that what we did that night was because of your playing around with a love potion."

"Love potion? What we had wasn't' no love potion. That was us, pure, sweet, honest sexy lovemaking. Plain and simple," Delmar said.

"Uh-huh," Tiara laughed out. "You ain't telling a lie on that one, Delmar. Gosh, how I remember the sweet part of that night. We were good together." She pushed the thoughts of his crazy acting ways later that same night from her mind.

"I can see what you're thinking, Tiara, I don't know what came over me the next day, when I began acting," he hesitated. "Well just plain stupid. I've got no excuses," he said, not wanting to tell her about the curse that they were under.

He paused long enough to collect his thoughts. "I'm gonna be honest with you Tiara. This isn't easy for me being without you night and day. All I can say is that I apologize for my actions that day. I guess if I had to give you an excuse I've been overworked and I'm also a little afraid."

"Afraid of what?"

"Afraid of what I'm feeling for you, Delmar said.

Tiara put down her fork and paid close attention, as she studied Delmar's face. The intensity she saw staring back at her was real. "Please tell me you're just teasing me."

"You'd like that?" He asked but didn't wait for her response. "I mean if you thought I was just joking around, but I'm not," he said reaching out to place his hand on top of hers. "You have no idea how much I ache to touch you, to hold you and yes to make love to you again."

There was an uncomfortable silence as Tiara looked across the table at Delmar and felt such a deep ache.

"I'm serious," Delmar said, staring back at her boldly.

"I'm sorry Delmar, but you caught me off guard. Hearing him say how much he wanted her had taken her by surprise. She felt an excitement began to build in her. She closed her eyes and let the feeling consume her.

He squeezed her hand leaned close and whispered. "I was wondering if we could, go somewhere," his fingers softly reached up her arm and caressed downward, slowly.

"Mmmm," Tiara moaned. His gentle fingers caressing her arm was doing things to her. She liked the feeling it gave.

Tiara opened her eyes smirking like a kid. "That sounds so fascinating. Where do you desire to take me?" She inquired with a dangerous gleam in her eyes.

Delmar whispered in a sexy cool hoarse voice. "Wouldn't it be nice to go someplace where we could make love again?"

Tiara giggled out a purr. "So that you can squeeze me real tight repeatedly, right? " She didn't wait for his response. "You know where that leads?"

"Why of course I do. You realize that's what I want. And I'm sure you'd love to make love to me again too," he murmured low and seductive.

"Damn, Delmar, you are bold as hell and you're right. I would love for you to make love me again?" She giggled.

Tiara knew she was dick whipped when it came to Delmar, but she wasn't any fool. She had a babysitter to pay for once she got home. Dare she recognized that once she stepped out of her Spinderella dressed-up and crossed the threshold of her front door, her time was no longer her own.

Tiara peered back at Delmar and let out a heavy sigh. "You know Delmar, I've got twins boys at home, a babysitter who wants to be paid and no room at my inn. If you know what I mean. Once I get home the twins will monopolies all of my time."

"Come on now, Tiara. We both know I'll pay the babysitter double even triple if you want me to. All you must do is agree to come with me. I'll get us a room at the best hotel in town, if you want me too. But you know I still have my penthouse," he kissed her hand. "Now beautiful lady, all you have to do is decide if you want me to screw you first. Or if you prefer me to work some magic with my tongue and get to kissing your pussy first," he paused to let his words sink in. "So, which one will you prefer I do, first.?"

Tiara giggled and blushed all at the same time and blurted. "I'll decide once we get where we are going. Okay, now Delmar, let's get out of here!"

***

Hours later, that same morning Tiara stood naked enjoying the rooftop panoramic views of the City of San Jose below. She'd forgotten Delmar kept the rooftop penthouse high above downtown San Jose.

She spun around and strolled back to the bed and stood above Delmar staring. He laid asleep on his stomach giving her a perfect view of his lean hard athletic body.

She inhaled in a deep breath remembering this was the body that had given her a workout sending her body into an insatiable frenzy while they were making love.

Tiara didn't know what came over her when she reached out her hand and ran it down the length of his back before settling on his skin-tight butt. So confident, that Delmar was still asleep. She softly whispered. "You are so irresistible."

"Thank you beautiful lady, I think you're irresistible too," he answered, his agile body quickly turning over. He reached up and grabbed her hands and pulled her down on top of him.

Instantly, Tiara straddled him and in one fluid motion, she sank down onto his erection.

She peered down at him thinking she should feel a shame for what she was doing. But she couldn't feel any shame. She only knew that there was no shame in how much she needed him to make love to her.

With his mouth, Delmar kissed a path to the deep valley of her breasts. "I don't want you to stop," he rasped.

"Don't worry, I won't," she replied, breathlessly, as she moved rhythmically up and down on top of him.

Staring up at Tiara straddling him. Delmar clenched his jaw. His last thought was it was much too late for both, destiny had sealed their fate and he was coming to grips with a real-life truth. He was in love with her.

Slowly he lay back and gazed into Tiara face and watched as it contorted with passion before he gave in and joined her in his need for sexual pleasure, as he let Tiara ride him in wave after wave of sexual pleasure as they climaxed together.

Chapter 14

In a dream

The knock at the bedroom door was soft and loud at the same time. Delmar looked over at Tiara, she was still sound asleep. He slipped out of bed, and snatched his shirt and headed for the door.

Nona stifled a giggled. "I see you've been busy," she said.

Delmar glanced down at his unbuttoned shirt. "How did you know I was here?"

Nona and Delmar traded looks.

Delmar shook his head. "Ignore that I asked that. "Why are you here?"

"We are on a quest, remember? We should have been gone hours ago," Nona replied.

"But... But, I have a guest."

"Don't I know it," Nona responded. "Here," she said putting some clothes in his hand. "Now, go and get a shower, and dressed."

In an instant, he noticed she was holding some women's clothes. "You're not thinking of waking…"

"Of course not, your guest isn't joining us. These clean clothes are for when she wakes up. Oh, and here," she answered shoving a letter into his hand. "Sign your name to this letter. I'll place it on top of the young woman's clothes so that she'll know that you just didn't abandon her."

Nona headed for the bedroom.

Delmar tensed. "No! Don't go in there. You might wake her."

"Oh, relax Delmar. Your young lady won't wake up, until after we leave. What do you take me for, an amateur?"

Nona walked into the bedroom and stood at the threshold staring back at Tiara. She took a calming breath and then said. "She's the young lady you're going through all of this for, isn't she?"

Delmar closed the distance between them. "Yes, she is." He was surprised Nona was blushing when she turned at looked at him.

Tiara's half her nude body was exposed from under the covers.

"Go on and get your shower," Nona replied, laying the woman's new clothes on a chair.

Delmar headed for the shower and then hesitated. "What's going to happen when she wakes up? I mean this wasn't just a dream, was it?"

Nona took another calming breathed. "When she wakes up all she will remember is that she had a good night's sleep. When it is time for her to remember that she was here with you. Don't worry, she will remember."

Chapter 15

Glenda, Jackson, Common and Fanny

A car engine backfiring startled Glenda as she strolled over to the window and peered out. She arrived just in time to see a huge smoky cloud. It vaporized like an apparition, but she saw no sign of a car. She thought it was weird as if she had called up the smoky apparition. The car sounded again. It was familiar. She wondered if the noise was coming from their backyard, was it from her garage. She seen her husband, Jackson, stroll out back earlier. In fact, he'd left the back door opened when he went out.

"Scott Irishman-Jackson, are you fumbling around with my automobile!" She wailed.

"Nay, love. I gained enough sense not to tinker with that old Cadillac of yours, that you love so much," Jackson answered, striding back inside. He was holding Pinky the cat.

Jackson stroked Pinky's coat as he closed the distance between them. "Did you hear that noise too?" He inquired but didn't wait for a reply. "It boomed like a car backfiring. But since I've been living with you all these years. I've learned that things that have to do with magic always sound like common ordinary things."

Glenda felt a small nagging feeling centered in the pit of her stomach. Something was coming.

As though looking for agreement, Jackson's eyes searched Glenda's. "I was right, you feel it too. Something good, bad or ugly is coming this way, shortly."

Glenda glared at Jackson. "You are right, Jackson. Even Pinky feels it. Look she's changed colors twice since you walked through the back door."

Pinky purred loudly and gave a mesmerizing stare. The family pet Pinky was a color changing cat a mixture of Siamese, Himalayan, and other Oriental cats, with a long history of having the ability to change colors.

The air around them felt strange.

Something was wrong.

Pinky purred loudly as if giving off a warning. Pinky gave her a mesmerizing stare into the middle of the room. No one was there.

Jackson's green eyes widened. "That's all the proof I need that you need to do a protection around us, now, and I do mean you, wife, Glenda D'Goodwrench-Jackson! Because we both know neither Pinky nor I have any such talents in this family."

"No, worries man, what do you think I've been doing?" Glenda replied.

All at once Glenda looked up and whooped, as she felt the air suck out of the room with a suction power so strong she wondered why it didn't leave the room looking like a tornado had smashed it.

A crack of thunder sounded loud then the utterly inexplicable happened. A spirit coughed fiercely and appeared.

"Hello, dearie, it is I, Common, and Fancy."

All at once Fancy stepped from behind Common giggled and walked over and plopped down on a bar stool.

"Is the bar closed?" Fancy inquired. "I'd sure like a drink. I toiled up such a thirst getting here."

Jackson idly walked over to his favorite place. "I'm honored to say, my bar is always opened, if I am around. What can I get for you?"

"I want something with the word virgin in it," Fancy giggled, with a gleam in her eye, staring back at Jackson, like he was a scoop of decadent ice cream. "Though I don't know why? I haven't been a virgin for years."

There was an odd look on Fancy's face as she took in Jackson's backside as he made her drink. The gleam was beautiful, strange, seductive.

As Glenda watched Fancy she shook out her thoughts, she wasn't sensitive to an overly flirting woman. Especially when it came to Jackson. He was loyal to her through and through. She knew nothing was going to happen between Fancy and Jackson when she turned and placed her attention on Common.

"So, Common, why are you here?"

He grinned, and he peeked back at Fancy and Jackson at the bar. "She is indeed harmless," he announced, letting his gaze linger on Fancy.

Glenda and Common had a brief exchange. "I'm not concerned about Fancy. I'm worried about why you are here," she answered.

"I'm… Um… I'm not good at lying," Common said. "And I was hoping to talk to you about something… Something odd that happened," he pondered. "Or something that I believe has happened."

Glenda crossed her arms over her chest. She was growing vexed with Common for taking his own sweet time. "Common are you going to get to the reason of why you are here? Or are you going to continue to talk in riddles?"

"It's hard to explain," he said. "I'm afraid we haven't been able to verify it yet. But it would seem, that when Delmar's ancestor came through the portal to help us know how to break the curse," he paused. "Well, it seems that someone or something may have come through with him."

"Oh!" Glenda replied. "So, if you don't know for certain if something came through the portal than are you using the services of a ghost hunter to find out?"

Common shook his head. "No," he stated not meeting her eyes. "We resolved not to engage a ghost hunter because it is a wild accusation by Delmar's relative, who has not produce any evidence that there was a breach in the portal when he accessed it."

Glenda took a deep breath. "Tell me all that you know Common."

"All, I simply know is that Delmar's ancestor said that he sensed a presence when he had entered the portal and when he left to return. But, whoever or whatever it was left behind no trace of their being there," Common added, cautiously. "I was sent to tell you so that you can warn Nona and Delmar to be careful, we don't know what we are dealing with."

Glenda could see Common was thoroughly concerned about something. His face showed concern. She exhaled. "It's not working," she declared. "I mean if you expect me not to be concerned you could at least hide that look of dread on your face. What is it you're are not telling?"

"I was hoping that you wouldn't ask," he said. "Oh, well it's just as well that you know what I have been thinking." He shifted his weight and lean in close so that only they could hear. "I have learned more about this thing between Delmar's ancestor and Tiara's. It seems that Delmar 's ancestor failed to inform us that he had cast a love spell upon Tiara's ancestor to force the girl to fall in love with him and marry him. Only thing is he thought he'd gave Tiara's ancestor the love potion but unbeknownst to him, the liquid in his bottle was nothing but sweet wine. He didn't know that someone close to him had stolen the bottle, with the real love potion and replaced it with the replica bottle containing the sweet wine that he'd gotten from the Hoodoo Queen, Marie Laveau."

"What?" Glenda inquired. "You can't know something like that? With such details, I mean and not no who performed the deed. Tell me at once."

Common looked more distraught than before. "Sadly, I do. The only problem is my source has not been able to help me determine if the love potion was stolen by a man or a woman."

Glenda looked back at Fanny and Jackson with keen interest. The greatest tragedy in life is when love is not returned. Since the dawn of time, love potions have been used to intoxicate an unsuspecting love interest, men and women have used it to change the course of their lives. She thought about adding a few drops of some into the glass of milk her husband Jackson always drank, just before going to bed. *Perhaps it would add a little spice to our love life,"* she pondered.

Glenda turned her attention back to Common and shook out her thoughts. "The best love potion contains an aphrodisiac of properties to lure in your lover. Perhaps Delmar's ancestor had a secret admire capable of doing the same thing as he. Maybe she or he stole the love potion."

"Perhaps you're right," Common said. "Or something else not of this world. You see, I've learned that Delmar's ancestor dabbled in all kinds of black magic in his time."

"Hmmm that is interesting," Glenda commented.

"I am willing to bet that when it is all said and done, we may learn that Delmar's ancestor's rise from property to riches was because he made a deal with Mr. D."

Glenda knew that many referred to the devil as Mr. D. "Mr.

D., isn't someone to do anything without a price."

"Yes, I agree and if Delmar's ancestor did have dealings with Mr. D…"

Common interrupted her. "Mr. D. would have extracted his payment immediately. Even if that payment meant death."

Glenda shivered as she nodded agreement. "Perhaps you are right."

A crack of thunder sounded loud as if giving off a warning.

Common looked back at Fancy sitting at the bar. He took a deep breath. "I'm afraid it is time that Fancy and I got going. We must get to Haiti as quickly as possible. Family duty calls and I must go."

Intrigued by his statement Glenda asked. "You have family in Haiti?"

Common clasped his hands and proudly stated. "Yes, there are still a few Ogun's around. We're to visit my brother Hercules Ogun and his family and our cousin Zaca Ogun, has promised to bring his family to the gathering."

He walked over to the bar where Fanny stood chitchatting with Jackson. "Fanny dear, it is time that we leave."

The sound of a car engine backfiring pierced the air as a cloud of fog appeared out of nowhere just as a loud crack of thunder sounded loudly, and then Common and Fanny vanished.

Glenda closed the distance between her and Jackson. She took a deep breath and said. "Jackson my love, why don't we turn in early tonight?"

"That sounds like a plan, love," Jackson said. "I'll go and make sure everything is locked-up tightly."

"Splendid idea and I'll go and fetch you a tall glass of ice cold milk just the way you like it."

"Oh, yes, Glenda darling you do know your Jackson well and you take really good care of me," Jackson smiled.

Chapter 16
White Witch of Antioch
Different but the same

The bright overhead moon gave off more than enough light when Nona and Delmar dropped down out of their travel portal onto the gravel trail.

Delmar took a deep breath as he touched down on the ground. He was starting to get used to this way of travel, as he glanced around and spotted some semi-steep hills and some semi-rough terrain surrounding them. Even in the late night, he could tell the place was beautiful. He noticed flowery fields, luminously beautiful in the darkness. He turned his head and saw some friendly cows standing proudly in the moonlight.

"Where are we again?"

"We're in the Black Diamond Mines Preserve, near Mount Diablo," Nona said, gesturing and making her way down the trial.

As he slipped in step behind her, Delmar started to think stories he had learned about the Black Diamond Mines. Mostly his stories were from when he was a kid and he'd learned it was one of the spookiest places in California. He recalled a story about another scary spot that was not far from where they were. It was referred to as the *Gates of Hell* because it was where an insane asylum was formerly located.

"Hey Nona, did you know that there was once an insane asylum not too far from here."

Nona paused and turned and faced him. "Of course, I did, Delmar, it was a great tragic monument of man's cruelty to man. With its straitjackets, shock treatments, and lobotomies. Thankfully, those brutal practices are no longer performed today."

"We can only hope," Delmar added and then asked curiously. "Do you really think a real witch lives in the cemetery?" he asked letting out a sigh. "I wonder what her story is?"

"Yes, I do, the *White Witch*, was told to be a midwife who was on her way to deliver a baby when her carriage fell over, and she was crushed to death," she hesitated.

Delmar rubbed his brow. "I suppose I'll find out, shortly if she's for real."

Curiously he paused and glanced around and noticed a huge hedge forest obscure the pathway in front of them. "We're supposed to find a cemetery here?"

Nona touched his arm and made him aware of where she was pointing. "We should find *Rose Hill Cemetery,* just beyond that hedge forest. Come, let's move on."

Once past the great hedge forest, they stepped into a clearing. It was picture perfect.

A celestial realm, stood before them, casting alight scene with as colorful night blooming flowers bordered the trail all around them.

Delmar took a deep breath and knew he was breathing in night candy. Known also as night phlox because it gave off a sweet fragrance reminiscent of freshly baked goods. He marveled at the shades of white, purple and maroon it gave off as it unfurled its pinwheel-shaped blooms all along the trail.

"This place is magnificent," Nona replied. "And its smell is so intoxicating. That sweet smell is…"

"Night candy," Delmar said interrupting her. "It's a favorite of mine."

"Mine too," Nona said as they strode on.

The shriek of a bat and an owl's hoot gathered in harmony with a chorus of crickets, playing a night song that filled the silence around them.

Intently, Delmar notices the vast array of fireflies, fluttered about as the stillness of the night crept in around them. When he looked up he saw the gated entrance of the cemetery. The graveyard with its huge white tombstones was just beyond.

He thought he was imagining things when a bright white light emerged from behind one of the tombstones and began to float down to the road.

The silence of the night was eerie with anticipation.

"Nona, do you see what I see?"

"Yes, it's her! Keep walking towards her, act unafraid."

"I think I'm going to need a formal introduction," Delmar

joked, as he nervously cleared his throat.

The bright glowing light floated closer.

They drew to a halt when the bright orb of light hovered directly in front of them.

"Nona?"

Delmar jumped at the sound of the voice that came from the bright light. It sounded like it had been right behind him instead of coming from the being in front of him.

"Yes, it is I," Nona said. "My friend, Delmar and I come in peace."

The White Witch hovered. "Lady Eidothea has told me of your coming. You seek the next item."

"Yes, we do, and the location of the place it will be found, Nona replied.

"The item that you seek is called the healing love herb, for it is a rare plant possessed of a soul that is sensitive and capable of vast healing."

Nona exhaled. "Of course, why hadn't I thought of it. Healers have been using the healing love herb in potions and tonics for centuries. Where can we find it?"

"Your quest will begin at the Diablo's cave, the healing love herb only grows there, you can't miss it." The White Witch said. " One of the passages ways in the cave is filled with it. And it has a distinct smell"

"Oh, yes it bears a rich caramel, vanilla and cherry smell that you can't miss," Nona replied.

The White Witch nodded approval. "Come, I will take you to the cave's opening."

Nona and Delmar walked side by side along the trail as they made their way out of the graveyard.

Delmar glanced back again and again as they made their way out of the graveyard. He had an eerie feeling that they were not alone.

Minutes later they past a forest next to a hillside with a steep canyon ravine next to it.

Before they could descend into the ravine, something caught Delmar's eye lying in the bushes. He stepped off the trial reached down and picked up a fresh looking backpack.

Nona stopped and gave Delmar a questioning glance and then realized what he had spotted. She observed as he unzipped the backpack and found that it contained a couple flashlights, some torches and other items needed to light your way into a tunnel or a cave.

"Well look at this?" Delmar stated as he reached Nona's side.

"It looks like luck is on our side," Nona replied. "The night fairies have provided backpacks for us."

"Or some unlucky person dropped their backpack," Delmar added.

The White Witch floated in front of them and came to a standstill in front of four great pine trees intertwined. They marked an entrance to a secret cavern.

"The entrance is just behind these trees," the White Witch said. "Follow me."

Instinctively, the White Witch skirted around and trees and floated in front of two large boulders that gave off the illusion of sealing off the cave.

"Just as we skirted past the trees, you must walk to the far end of the boulder and you will see the cave's entrance. I must leave you here but once you return I will be waiting."

She drifted over to Nona and Delmar. "Let me caution you that once inside Diablo's cave strange things may happen. Some say it is because of the strange gases that the caves give off that makes folks act strange or see things, but whatever you do. Remember it's not real."

Delmar snorted. "What do we do now? Go inside?"

The White Witch ignore Delmar's questions. "Oh, and Delmar don't forget, you must not disturb the healing love herb. Only Nona's hands may touch it. Diablo's cave is not that big, but it has a few passageways. Two are dead ends and two connect with each other. The only trouble is there is no way for me to identify you which passageway is which, so be careful."

A long moment passed.

Nona touched Delmar's shoulder. "Come on, Delmar, we don't have all night."

She moved to the end of the large boulder. The opening was just as the White Witch had said. She slipped inside

Delmar followed closely behind. They entered an enormous circular chamber with a flat stone floor. Just as the White Witch had stated, several passageways descended off the massive chamber.

"Give me a flashlights Delmar," Nona replied.

Delmar did as Nona instructed and let out a heavy sigh and stared surprised. "Which passage do we take first?"

Nona turned and glanced at him. "Delmar, I was thinking that we each take one passage, we can find the healing herb quicker. If you find a plant growing in the walls of the cave with a rich caramel, vanilla, and cherry like the fragrance that'll be our healing love herb. Just don't touch it. Come and get me, okay?"

Delmar was barely listening to her as he took out his flashlight and made sure it was working. He headed to the passageway closest to him.

At first, there was plenty of light in the passage. But as time went on the passageway got darker and darker.

It was curiously silent except for a peculiar hissing sound. Suddenly Delmar felt tiny drops of mist touch his skin. He wiped his brow and felt the moisture with his fingertips and then touched one of his fingertips to his tonque. It tasted sweet.

Delmar lost track of time. He only knew that he was deep in the passage and the darkness was all around him.

Out of the corner of his eye, he thought he caught the glimpse of a dark figure running in the darkened passageway. He felt a cold flutter in the pit of his stomach as he watched a dark figure, dart quickly in front of him and dashed away.

The air felt weird.

Startled Delmar called out. "Is someone there? Who are you?"

He gasped as a figure came into view. It was a woman. She looked like Tiara.

"Tiara?" Puzzled he mumbled and suddenly thought to himself. *"What was it that the White Witch had said, nothing is real."*

Just then something totally unexpected happened. The figure that was Tiara cloned itself and two Tiara's stood before Delmar.

He gasped in surprised bewilderment.

Amazed he couldn't believe it was his voice. "Tell me, which one of you is my Tiara?"

"I am!" Tiara to the left spoke in a silvery voice.

"Don't trust him!" Tiara to the right yelled in a disembodied penetrating voice. "This man is a fool! A fool who cannot be trusted. He will use you! His kind always does."

Delmar felt his headache as he looked back at the two Tiaras. Tiara on the left eyes was tearing up. The look in her eyes broke his heart. He nodded at her just before he squeezed his eyes shut trying to stop the ache in his head.

"Delmar, I won't listen to her," her sweet silvery quiver voice said. "I believe in you. I am the one who truly loves you... Please, Delmar, save us!"

The Tiara on the right hissed out in an awful scream. "Shut up! You foolish girl!"

Suddenly Tiara on the right floated over to Tiara on the left, lifted her hand and struck her across the face.

"Stop!" Delmar yelled in a whisper, gasping for air, helpless to intervene.

Tiara on the right screamed in agony as she crumpled to the floor.

"Can't you see Delmar has never loved you!" Tiara on the right scolded her. "He never could, and he never will!"

Even with his head pounding Delmar knew it was the Tiara on the left who was speaking. She had a deep-seated hatred for him. He could feel it deep in his core.

Suddenly he opened his eyes and met the eyes of Tiara on the left, lying on the ground. Her eyes met his and pleaded with him. He watched her lips as they mouthed a plea.

"Delmar please save us!"

He loved her. He felt it deep in his bones. He cleared his throat and blurted. "I love you Tiara! Hold on I'm going to save you. I never want to lose you. Heaven knows I am trying to save us both!"

"I know you love me, Delmar, as I love you," Tiara on the left mouthed to him. "But she is afraid of death, she is afraid to pass on to the next dimension," she said looking at the other Tiara.

"You liar!" Tiara on the right disembodied penetrating voice screamed back at her Tiara sister. "You, stupid fool! He will destroy us! But I will kill you first before I let him!"

Out of thin air, she produced a knife and wheeled back her arm, just as she dies all at once a brilliant pink light rose up out of nowhere and she dropped the knife and vanished into the darkness.

"Delmar!" Nona yelled, "Delmar, where are you?"

"Nona... Nona! I'm over here!" He called in a raspy voice.

Nona aimed her flashlight towards the sound of Delmar's voice and rushed over. She crouched down beside him. "Delmar are you alright?"

After a long pause, their eyes meet. "What happened to you, Delmar?" Nona asked.

Delmar continued to look back into Nona's face for a long time until recognition registered. He could barely breathe. "Nona? Nona? Is that really you?"

With a huge effort, Delmar tried to raise up. But quickly laid back down. His eyes wide. He looked around for the two Tiaras.

He took a deep breath and looked around. "Nona, did you see them? Is she alright?"

"See who?" she asked, curiously.

"The two Tiaras," Delmar said, as he drew another deep breath.

Nona frowned. The surrounding vibrations around her were strained, she felt something had transpired before she found Delmar lying on the ground. She needed to get the two of them out of the cave."

"Delmar, how do you feel? Are you injured?"

He shook his head. "No, I just couldn't breathe and the next thing I noticed I went down to the ground."

"Here, let me help you up," Nona said, pulling Delmar's arm around her neck. "Now, lean on me for support. We have to get out of here."

Delmar did as he was instructed, and he and Nona slowly shuffled back in the direction he had come.

A short time later, the two of them stepped out of the Diablos cave.

Looking over his shoulder Delmar spotted the White Witch floating over.

"Is he alright?" The White Witch asked.

"That's an excellent question," Nona replied. "He seems to be, but I think he may have encountered some of that gas that you mentioned. I found him lying on the cave's floor, hallucinating."

Slowly Delmar straightened and glanced around. He strolled back toward the path they had entered and suddenly turned and stared back at the entrance of Diablo's cave. Being deep inside that passageway had been like descending into an old nightmare. A dream that had followed him across time.

He kept thinking back to his childhood. Thinking about all the things his father didn't do for him. Fathers were supposed to lead the way. Teach their children how to be better people than they were. His father had been rich, and he brought him things and gave him things none of which was what he'd really needed in life. Now the thought that he could lose the one thing he now knew was most important in life. Filled him with a great sadness. He'd failed.

A hush settled around them.

The White Witch floated over to Delmar. "They say true love is the greatest weapon," she said.

"I am a lost man without purpose, without focus, without devotion and sometimes I feel without hope," Delmar mumbled.

"Ahhhh, but redemption is always willing to be a friend," The White Witch said.

"Redemption isn't looking for me, as a friend," Delmar shrugged. "I'm falling short not to mention falling down on the job too, just look at me. I'm dirty, I'm hungry and I failed to find the healing love herb. Therefore, I have failed."

The White Witch floated around in a dance and then came to a halt. "Redemption can be as simple as just changing your life to do the right thing instead of the wrong thing. Time and patience are all that you need Delmar, except maybe for a strong glass of whiskey to warm your bones, and a little faith, to mend your soul."

The White Witch spun around and saw where Nona was standing. "Nona!" she called.

Startled Nona looked up from where she was squatting. "Yes, what is it?" She asked retrieving the backpack.

"Don't you have something to share with Delmar?"

"What?" Nona asked.

The White Witch floated over to Nona's side. "He doesn't know that you were successful in your quest."

"I'm so sorry, Delmar!" Nona said, rushing over. "I have the healing love herb. I placed it in that backpack of yours. Why do you think I've been keeping it so close?"

Delmar reached over and gave Nona a hug. "Thank you!" he murmured fiercely. "All is not lost."

The White Witch floated around in a dance and leveled in front of Delmar and Nona. "Now, it is time for you to know where to go for your next item," she said. "In seven days' time the new moon will be directly overhead, then you must go then to see Queen Calafia, the Black Queen of California. She lives in Pluto's cave at Mount Shasta.

"The Black Queen," Delmas said bewildered. "I've never heard of such..."

"Queen Calafia is whom this great state of California is named after," The White Witch fiercely said interrupting him.

Nona frowned. "There are a lot of things you don't know Delmar. They aren't printed in a school book nor taught."

The White Witch's laughter filled the air. "How can one explain such things to mortal man? Queen Calafia is a most powerful queen who still rules this state, even in death. For you see Delmar, death is only a change in location."

Nona didn't say anything just smiled and looked at Delmar. What could she say to him to make him understand? She took a deep breath and cut a glance at the White Witch. She could tell that the White Witch wasn't done giving Delmar a history lesson.

The White Witch floated in close to Delmar. "I suppose you believe in history, right Delmar?"

"Yes," he responded.

"Then I'm sure you will find reading a book called *The Adventures of Esplandián*, fascinating. It was written in 1500. In it you will read that the crusader and conqueror Hernán Cortés led an expedition to the land of Calafia or California, where he discovered a land of natives, of Moors, Black Native American and Red Native American and met the courageous regal black woman, who ruled over the land of California, named Calafia."

At that moment, Delmar realized he'd been a stupid fool all his life. He had to admit to himself he knew nothing. About California history or women for that matter. There was a lot he had to learn. He drew a deep breath and established eye contact with Nona. "Can we go now? I feel like I can do with that strong glass of whiskey now."

Chapter 17
Whiskey, Wine & Women!

Tiara laid across her bed numb. She couldn't believe her twin sons had finally fallen asleep. Now was her time to take a much-needed nap.

She had just slipped off into a deep sleep when she heard the phone beside her bed start to ring. She struggled to ignore it but by the third ring she reached over and picked it up.

"Hello."

"Hi Tiara, it's me, Zack."

Zackary Vaughn and Tiara had always been an on again off again item for the past few months. She hadn't heard from Zack since that night they went dancing and he had to leave and take an emergency to the hospital.

"How are you Zack," Tiara asked, leaning back on her bed thinking sometimes the reality of a fantasy can sneak right up and pinch you on the behind. Sometimes you just wanted a guy to hold you.

"I'm good," he breathed. "I was hoping to take you out, have dinner go dancing, you know have some fun."

As he spoke, a smile rose on her face. It was what she wanted to sometimes just going out and getting around from the mommy thing was just what she needed. Sometimes you just wanted a guy to hold you.

"Mmmm, sounds like you are reading my mind, Zack," she hesitated. "But I don't have a babysitter, looks like I'm stuck inside for the night."

"Don't say that I'm sure Odessa Johnson's granddaughter Linda Perrin, is available."

Tiara laughed. "This sounds so familiar. You wouldn't by chance already have spoken to Odessa or Linda?"

Zack laughed into the phone. "You know me, of course, I did. Now how long do you need to get dressed."

Five hours later that night, Tiara wondered what the hell was wrong with her going out with Zackary Vaughn. He wasn't a bad guy, but after a few drinks he really started looking like the right guy. How would she feel if she gave this man her goodies all the while her heart was with Delmar? She knew she was a weak woman. She had never felt so frustrated in all of her life.

She closed her eyes and let her thoughts fill with the memories of Delmar and their early years together. Her feelings for him was strong. She thought about Delmar wrapping his arms around her. She thought about the love she had for him. She thought about the fear he would never want to have anything to do with her if she slept with Zack.

Tiara shivered at the thought of losing Delmar and it woke her out of her head. She took a sip of the Patron and winced. She put the drink down. She felt her head slamming. A headache was coming on. She wondered if she had too much to drink. She needed to get some air.

"Excuse me, Zack, I need to go to the ladies' room," she said, clutching her purse and quickly heading for the lady's room.

Someone sailed past her just as she opened the bathroom door. "Pardon me, coming through," the familiar voice spoke bluntly.

"Diademe?"

"Oh, it's you, Tiara, please excuse my rudeness, I was anxious to go," Diademe blew air through her teeth.

Tiara didn't dare look into her eyes. Her head was hurting badly. "Hi, Diademe, nice to see you again."

"Tiara, my friend," Diademe said with sugary tenderness in her voice, "I was starting to worry that I wouldn't see you again. I've missed our conversations. Where are you sitting, do you mind if I join you?"

It was a tension-filled moment.

"I... Uh..."

"Tiara, you don't look well," Diademe reported. "Should I be concerned? Do I need to call someone?"

Tiara's pulse pounded, as she put her hand to her forehead. "I could use your help, I'm not feeling well."

Diademe gave Tiara a malevolent grin. "Here, lean on me, Tiara, I'll make sure you are taken care of," she hesitated and murmured under her breath. *"I'm going to take really proper care of you."*

Twenty minutes later, Diademe couldn't believe how easy it had been to get Tiara out of her favorite black dress and put her in a cab to take her home. But before she did she made sure she gave Tiara a good dose of a dreamless sleeping potion. Tiara wouldn't remember a thing once she woke up.

Transforming into a human woman wasn't hard for Diademe, it was necessary and an added sweet indulgence. Besides, she could experience the world like Tiara.

She headed back to Tiara's and Zack's table. There sat Zack eagerly waiting for her return.

Zack had thought Tiara was breathtakingly beautiful when he first brought her to the club hours ago, but now after she spent almost a half hour in the bathroom, she was looking resplendently stunning in her favorite black dress.

"Wow! You look amazing," Zack said, as Tiara came back to their table.

"Thank you," Diademe stated in her finest Tiara voice. "May I have a glass of whiskey, straight?" She knew she was always the smart one, it wouldn't take her long to figure out how to get Zack exactly where she desired him, in bed, giving her what she hadn't had in hundreds of years. She smiled with anticipation and licked her lips.

She chatted idly with Zack and made it a point to laugh on and off at things that he said. When her drink came, she tossed it back and demanded another one.

Since being back on earth she had a chance to read a couple of those romance novels where the good men were always intelligent, with gorgeous male muscles, and at least eight inches in the male equipment department, sitting there looking at Zack she wondered if he had eight inches, she hoped for more. She licked her lips.

"You know Zack, I have a sixth sense, she said.

"What?" he asked, with a chuckle.

"Yes, I'm clairvoyant. You know that sixth sense thing where you can pick up the thoughts of others," she purred. "I'm picking up that you really want to relax, more."

Zack chuckled. "That's true. That's why I'm out right now, with you."

Diademe stared back at Zack, realizing how stupid he was. It was evident he didn't have a clue about what she was talking about. She exhaled slowly and then replied. "It's obvious Zack, you lack the intellectual capacity to understand what I'm saying. Let me put it into words I read in one of the earth's romance novels perhaps than you'll understand."

She leaned a crossed the tabled and purred. "Zackary, can't you see that I want you? Real bad? Real... Real bad!"

"Wow, I've never seen you act like this before Tiara," Zack murmured. "There's something different about you."

Diademe laughed hearing Zackary think that she was Tiara. Everything was working out like she planned. "Don't you want to make me cum, Zackary?"

Zack looked at Tiara, surprised by the words she was using. Tiara never spoke to him that way.

"Yesssss!" he moaned.

"Don't you think we should get out of here?" Diademe said, mimicking Tiara's voice to perfections.

They rose laughing together and headed door the corridor to the exit.

From across the room, Delmar watched them. He saw when Tiara and Zack rose to leave.

Just before they made it to the exit door, *Diademe-Tiara* pushed Zack against the wall and ran hands up and down his body.

Zack laughed wildly and brought his head close to hers. "If you ask me to kiss you right now, I will."

Delmar watched safely from a distance. He couldn't stand watching Tiara and Zack together. He stepped from where he'd been hiding and went to cross the room. Just as he did he collided with someone.

"Delmar! Thank God, I found you. You're not going to believe this…"

"Camille! Eris! What are you doing here?"

Camille strolled up quickly and stood in front of Delmar. "Somethings in life are hard to explain," she answered. "Some things we know for sure are real and some things are just an illusion."

"Yeah, like safety and love," Eris quickly added.

"Eris!" Camille interrupted.

"Well, hell love is an illusion it can quickly slip through anyone's grip, I'm just saying."

The moment was awkward.

"What say you buy us a drink, Delmar?" Eris asked.

"Eris, stop being so forward," Camille replied.

"Look, there's no room for cowards in my life," Eris said. "Come on Delmar, take us to the bar, we are thirsty!"

As they headed for the bar, Camille leaned over and whispered in Eris' ear. "This plan of yours had better work."

"Don't worry it'll work," Eris whispered. "All we have to do is make sure Delmar gets good and drunk and forgets he saw Tiara leaving with Zackary and I've got something in my purse that says that he will."

Chapter 18

Kicked by a mule!

Later that same night, Diademe decided her night of passion in the bedroom with Zack was a tremendous letdown. She couldn't believe what she had discovered. No wonder the man was unmarried. *What earth bound woman would put up with that in the bedroom? Talk about deformed, the man's penis couldn't have been more than three inches long,* she thought as she left his downtown Condo and walked down the street. She had a good mind to think of a curse to put on him. But knew Mother Nature had already performed her best curse by equipping him with very little in the male's organ department.

Having transferred herself into human form, limited the way she could travel. She looked down at the high heels she was wearing and realized her feet were hurting. This human shoe wearing thing wasn't fun.

Moments later a taxi pulled up to the curb. "It's awfully late Miss, do you need a taxi?" The driver asked.

Diademe turned and faced the driver and smiled. She knew exactly where she wanted to go. "Yes, I do," she said, as she got in. Her thoughts raced, the first plan of business was to find Delmar Devereaux. She knew exactly where to go.

Fifteen minutes later she took the elevator to the top floor and took in the gorgeous rooftop panoramic view of the City of San Jose below. She walked up to the door and pushed the bell.

Inside his penthouse, Delmar was sprawled on the sofa, he'd just made it home.

The bell pealed again, and Delmar jumped off the sofa and walked to the door. He glanced through the security window.

Diademe looked up and Delmar's face was staring back at

her from the door window.

Staring back at her through the window. Delmar had an odd feeling. He blinked twice to make sure it was her. It was her, Tiara, he thought back to earlier, at the club, when he'd seen her leaving the club with Zack.

"Hi Delmar, it's me Tiara, can I come in?"

He opened the door. "Tiara? He asked curiously looking up and down at her.

Delmar thought something felt strange. He couldn't put his finger on it. He knew the dress was Tiara favorite black dress, because he'd seen her wear it before, but something just wasn't right. He shook out his thoughts.

"Tiara, please come in."

Instantly *Diademe* jumped into his arms. "I'm so sorry Delmar, I was such a fool for leaving with Zack. I can only say that I was just trying to make you jealous," her words tumbled out in rapid explosion. "It's only you that I want, please me love to me Delmar!"

She kissed him passionately.

Startled at first, Delmar didn't know what to make of it. Something felt different. Tiara's kiss didn't feel the same.

Moments later, abruptly Delmar stopped and sucked up air trying to catch his breath. He pushed Tiara out of their embrace and looked her dead in the eye. He could have sworn he saw something strange. Tiara's eyes were empty and something else. They looked dead.

He saw Tiara shiver with fear as he looked her over.

Seconds went by and then he said the most startling thing, in clear plain English, but didn't feel his lips move. He wondered if he was a ventriloquist. "You know Tiara, I've known you an awfully long time but this is the first time I felt the need to tell you that in a former life I was an earth bound devil, but now I'm just a man, with a higher calling," he quietly laughed. "Yet still I have this strange ability to see things, just like the devil. And right now I don't see a single thing about you that is beautiful to me. In fact, you look disgusting and sad."

Diademe couldn't believe this was happening. Seeing the look on Delmar's face made her feel like someone had just gave her an ass whooping. She opened her mouth to try and say something, but no sound came out. Someone had placed a protective spell around Delmar, she was sure of it.

"Look, Tiara! I... I don't know what's wrong. I just sense something ain't right and I can't do this. You madam need to leave."

Diademe's eyes widened. At least he still believed she was Tiara, she thought as she slowly backed away from Delmar and edged toward the door. Once she reached it, she flung it opened and flew out without so much as a whisper.

Delmar stood there staring after her trying to figure out what had just happened. He felt deeply confused before he realized he felt like his stomach was hurting. He felt like he'd been kicked by a mule.

Chapter 19

That Ain't Right!

That afternoon the next day, Camille glanced at her office phone again. "What is taking Eris so long to call?" She wondered. Eris had advised her she'd be in a meeting all morning and would call her as soon as she could.

All at once the front doorbell of her downtown office sounded. Camille remembered her coworker, Jane Chu had locked the front door when she left for lunch. It couldn't be her returning because she had her own key. Quickly, Camille rushed down the hallway to see who it was. She hesitated at the front door and peeped through the peephole and saw Eris standing there.

Frantically she opened the front door. "Eris, girlfriend, I thought you were going to call."

Eris strolled inside and quickly closed the door behind her. "This was too serious for me to call," she spewed out. "Besides aren't you glad to see me?"

"Well, yes, but I'm worried about Tiara and what we are going to do?"

"That's why I came over," Eris revealed. "There is no reason for us to be speaking about this over the phone. This situation calls for action. I suggest we go over to Tiara's and discover what's going on."

"Confront her about seeing her smooching all over Zackary and later leaving with him. First, she's going to think we were spying on her."

Eris snorted. "We weren't spying on her. It was just a fluke that we were there."

Camille studied Eris for a minute. "Coincidence my foot. We need a better lie than that."

Eris stiffened. "That's our story and we are sticking to it," she paused. "Well, what do you prefer us to say?"

"I don't know. What's wrong with the truth?" Camille

suggested but didn't wait for a response. "We tell her the truth. That we are aware she has been sleeping with Delmar because she told us and now we see her having some kind of torrid love affair with Zack! And that ain't right."

Eris shook her head in agreement. "No, that ain't right! Come on Camille, let's go! We got business with Ms. Tiara!"

"Oh, alright. But I have to lock up first, I'm the only one in the office today, everyone but Jane Chu and myself, went to a conference in Sacramento and I kind of recall Jane Chu telling me not to expect her back after lunch."

***

An hour later, Camille and Eris sat at Tiara's dining room table, sipping tea, and throwing each other nervous glances as they sat and munched on pecan scones.

Eris leaned in close to Camille and whispered."Well, when are you going to say something?" She whispered.

Camille's eyes widen. "Me? This was your plan."

Just at that moment Tiara reentered the room with a fresh pot of tea, and headed over. She leaned over and poured Camille a fresh cup of tea.

"Tiara dear, just half a cup for me," Camille said. "I've already had two cups." She nudged Eris.

"Okay," Tiara smiled and turned and begin to fill Eris' teacup.

"Oh, Tiara," Eris blurted. "Have you stop seeing Delmar? I mean are you going to tell him you're now interested in Zack?"

Tiara was dumbfounded. She halted in mid-pour and placed the teapot on the table and sat down. "Okay, you two. What is this about? This little visit is a charade."

Camille sighed and stole a glance at Eris. "What? I mean. We don't know what you're talking about."

"Yeah, Tiara what are you talking about?" Eris asked, nervously wiping scones crumbs off her face.

Tiara took a deep breath. "So, you're telling me you both just dropped by, out of the blue, to enjoy a cup of tea," she stared at them. "You two are poor liars, I'm just saying. Guilt is written all over your faces," she said shaking her head.

Eris wipe the corners of her mouth slowly. Feeling like she should divert the blame from herself. She didn't want any beef with Tiara. She cleared her throat loudly and said. "I told Camille you'd see through us. I told her to tell you the truth, but nay, she said let's do it her way."

Camille snorted out a laugh and with a hint of cynicism in her voice said. "Eris! You are such a storyteller. If I wasn't such a nice person. I'd slap the crap out of you right now. I'm the one who said tell Tiara the truth."

"I'd like to see you try. You never could fight Camille," Eris declared. "Remember who saved your butt from getting your ass-kicked in junior high?"

"Okay, you two knock it off. You two always do this when you get caught, trying to divert me off the subject. Stop it!" Tiara commanded. "Now! I demand the truth."

Camille turned and face Tiara. "Okay, Tiara, the truth is we saw you leaving the club the other night with Zack. Even though you knew Delmar was at the club waiting for you."

"What? No way! I knew I was looking for what you two were up to, but I wasn't looking to find a truckload of shit," Tiara grasped her mouth opened. "You have to be making this crap up."

"Well, you know what they say, when you look for shit, you'll find it," Camille blurted. "And looks like you been stepping in some real mile high shit, named Zackary Vaughn and without thigh high boots, I might add."

"Yeah, girlfriend! You where seen! Caught right in the act without your thigh high boots on," Eris repeated. "In fact, , if you ask me. You were snuggled up so close to Zack that you looked like you were a vampire trying to get a blood fix before the break of daylight. Now explain that!"

Tiara cut her eyes between her two best friends. She saw the seriousness on their faces and knew they were not making it up. "Trust me when I say I had no knowledge that Delmar was coming to the club. And most importantly I never left with Zack."

Tiara felt like she needed a drink and snatched a clean teacup and poured. She took a big swallow and felt the effects of the warm liquid glided down the back of her throat and she swallowed hard and said. "I couldn't have taken off with Zack, all I recall is that I was sent home in a taxi, babbling and without my favorite dress. I know because Linda Perrin, Odessa Johnson's granddaughter, was babysitting for me that night, and she met me at the door and paid my cab fare."

Dumbfounded, Camille and Eris exchanged glances. The moment was silent.

Tiara slipped a loose strand of hair behind her eye and broke the ice. "I must have been in bad shape that night because Linda put me to bed and stayed. She informed me in the morning that I was in no condition to get up and take care of the twins if they woke up in the middle of the night. And that's why she stayed."

Camille nodded. "I'm so glad Linda stayed. It sounded like you were in pretty bad shape."

"I was, I was babbling some crazy gibberish," Tiara replied looking crushed. "All I know is that I felt weird for a few days after."

Camille looked back at her friend with deep concern. It was clear something had happened to Tiara. She reflected back to the time Delmar had drugged her and she didn't know it. Now it seems as if someone had done the same to her best friend Tiara. She didn't give it a thought when she added. "Perhaps someone slipped something into her drink?"

Tiara leaned back in the chair and crossed her arms. "I thought of that but I never left Zack's side that night for one minute. I would have seen or remembered something."

"Then I suppose it couldn't have been Zack putting something your drink," Camille stated biting her lip remembering back to a time a long time ago. When Delmar was capable of doing that and so much more. Still, she knew Zack was a medical professional, but she recalled an article she read in the newspaper about medical professionals acting unethically. She wondered if Zack was capable of doing such a thing.

Tiara got up and started pacing. "I can understand what you are thinking Camille. But I never left Zack alone at the table. I would have noticed if he tried to spike my drink."

"I was thinking the same thing too," Eris added. "You know Delmar was a bit of a bad character not too long ago. Who's to say what Zack is capable of? He could do the same thing?"

"Yes, I can see both of your concerns. We all know what Delmar Deveraux was capable of in the past. But that was before Delmar changed. Yet, Zachary Vaugh, he's never given me any indication he's capable of doing a thing like that."

Tiara stood fixed in one spot as if willing herself to try and remember. Slowly she clenched her hand. "All I remember is that the next morning, my head felt funny and weird but I insisted that Linda drive me back to the club to get my car. I could never figure out what happened to my favorite dress."

Camille saw the worried look on Tiara's face and knew she was telling the truth. "You mean to tell me someone stole your favorite black Latin swing dress? The one you always loved to go dancing in?"

"Yes, now do you believe me? I never saw Delmar that night," Tiara shrugged, and strolled over ant took a seat back at the table. "Strange things have been happening to me lately, and I don't know why."

"That's deep!" Eris said. "If someone stole my favorite dress I hunt the heifer down and kick her ass."

"Never mind the dress, Eris. I just thought about something you two did," Tiara said. "What the hell were you and Camille doing in the club that night?"

"Obviously catching you leaving with Zack after he must have sneaked you a mickey or that new date rape drug," Eris replied. "Even if you say he didn't, how else can you explain it?"

"Trust me," Tiara blurted. "Zack couldn't give me a strong enough anything to follow that little teeny weeny penis man home."

"Whoa! Zack got a tiny penis?" Eris laughed. "Dawg! Are you serious? How long is it?"

"I believe he told me it was three inches. Why do you think he always wants to take me out? I don't judge him. I don't have sex with him either, but what of it?"

Eris smirked out laughing.

Camille watched Eris gnawed on that news like a starving dog with a bone. She'd have to talk to Eris about that later. Now, something more pressing was nagging at her attention. Tiara said weird things had been happening to her lately. She remembered back to that morning she picked her up at the coffee shop at the Fairmont Hotel, something peculiar had happened to Tiara that morning too. She loudly cleared her throat. "Tiara, I can't get this thought out of my head. You said weird things keep happening to you lately, and that night at the club, Eris and I really thought we saw you leave with Zack. What do you think is going on?"

"I don't know," Tiara shrugged.

"Camille where are you coming from with this?" Eris stated.

"I think that there is more to this than we can comprehend," Camille answered as she leaned forward in her chair. "Let me present it another way. Do these bizarre occurrences seem like they are man-made dramas or supernatural dramas?"

They all became silent. No one moved. The three friends stared between each other.

Finally, Tiara broke the ice. "It's strange that you say that. Weird things have been happening since you picked me up that morning from the Fairmont Hotel. I can't put my finger on it. But if I had to guess. I'd say it's surreal like, you know that supernatural stuff like Grand-mere Catherine, knows about."

Eris blurted. "Grand-mere who?"

"You remember Lacey La Cour's grandmother?" Camille added. "Mrs. Catherine Marie Rousseau-La Cour?"

"They affectionately call her Grand-mere Catherine," Tiara anxiously replied. "She regularly goes to bingo with Camille's mother Gabby."

"Oh, yeah. The Bingo Queens' BFF posse. Grand-mere Catherine is the tall slender elegant looking woman that reminds you of royalty, she's the one," Eris smiled. "I always did like her. I think she knows my father."

"I admire them, the BFF posse, you know being best friends forever," Camille replied.

"Just like us," Tiara declared. "We're all life long, BFFs too, you know."

The three friends peered at each other and nodded agreement.

All at once Camille sat up straight, her eyes flashed as she flipped her hair. "I've got a great idea. I know who can tell us why all this strange stuff is happening to Tiara."

Eris tilted her head. "Who!"

"That's whom!" Tiara added.

Camille paused and took a long moment before answering. "Grand-mere Catherine was born with the gift of second sight. She's clairvoyant. She'll help us."

Eris gasped, and her mouth fell open.

Tiara eyed both her friends. "So, you think, Grand-mere Catherine, can help?"

Camille nodded. "I do."

Tiara leaned back in her chair. Her back stiffened. "Okay, then it's worth a try. I say we go see her."

Chapter 20

To many fools

Later that evening, Tiara couldn't get the thought that Delmar had seen her leave with Zackary Vaughn out of her head. She wondered if he'd thought she and Zack had a love connection. Little did he know that it was far from the truth. Still, if perception was reality then she didn't want Delmar's mind plagued with a false sense of reality.

But correcting things with Delmar would have to wait, as she watched as Camille drove her car along the curved country roads high above Alum Rock Park in the East San Jose hills known as Mount Hamilton.

The road afforded some of the best spectacular views of the city of San Jose spawned out at the bottom of the mountain as well as clear views of the sky high above the city.

In the distance, Tiara could see ominous clouds rolling in from the direction of the Pacific Ocean. She recalled back to her days in school and started counting one-one thousand, two-one thousand, three-one thousand…Boom! Lightning flashed. Light traveled faster than sound. She could tell the storm was miles away.

Tiara watched as Camille slowed down to turn onto the private road that held the La' Cour's family home. The home could be called a mansion. It sat on forty acres off the road.

A few minutes later, Camille pulled into the driveway and they watched as Grand-mere Catherine smiled as she strolled toward them.

"Welcome! Welcome!" Grand-mere Catherine greeted them. "Camille, your mother Gabby has been ringing my phone every ten minutes checking to see if you made it safe. She was afraid you get scared driving that curvy twisty mountain road."

"I was fine, and I loved the views," Camille said. "I think my mother has forgotten I've driven up her a few times in the past."

"You know how mothers are?" Grand-mere Catherine explained. "It's their right to worry about their young," she grinned. "And this must be your friend Tiara?"

"Yes, I'm Tiara Blake, I met you a long time ago."

"Hi Tiara," Grand-mere Catherine responded. "And you are Eris Simeon. You got your fathers eyes. I recognize those Simeon eyes, anywhere."

"Everyone always says that," Eris replied. "Nice to meet you again, Grand-mere Catherine."

"Now you tell your father I said hello, Eris," Grand-mere Catherine added. "He and my son Louis were the best of friends, back in their young days. God rest his soul."

"Yes, I remember. I will tell him, Grand-mere Catherine," Eris said.

"Oh, I just remember you three as young girls, you came to a few of my granddaughter Lacey La Cour's parties back when you were all teenagers," she exhaled. "That was a lot of years ago. Did you know my Lacey married Kienan Egan?"

"Everybody knows that." The three friends all spoke at once.

Instantly the fragrant aroma of the sausage laced gumbo filled the air.

"Mmmm something sure smells really good," Tiara commented.

"I smell it too," Eris added. "Gosh, that smell makes me hungry."

The embarrassing loud gurgling sound of an empty stomach pierced the air.

Everyone giggled.

"Sounds like somebody is hungry. You young ladies follow me into the house. I got a kettle-pot of Gator Gumbo ready on the stove in the kitchen."

Tiara's back stiffened as she fell alongside Camille and whispered. "Do you think she's serious? About the Gator in the Gumbo thing, I mean."

"Well, you just have to stick around and find out," Camille said in a hushed voice.

Minutes later, they enter the big spacious house. It had the feel of one of those homes you'd see in the Southern Living magazine.

They glanced around. The house was furnished with

beautiful furniture. Old and new and expensive.

Tiara was glad for her home furnishing training. She identified a few antiques. She knew they were good pieces, real and expensive.

"Gosh, this place reminds me of my great grandma's back home in Arkansas," Camille added.

"Yeah, I can feel the down-home warmth bringing back my childhood memories," Tiara smiled. "Makes you want to have a kitchen just like this one."

All three friends nodded in Unisom, as they entered the big spacious kitchen. It was warm, bright and made you feel welcomed.

Grand-mere Catherine's eyes sparkled as she washed her hands and quickly went about ladling up a large serving bowl of something piping hot.

"You three can use the sink to wash your hands, while I put supper on the table."

Minutes later the four of them were sitting at the table.

"Eat up ladies, we've got piping hot bowls of Gator gumbo, grilled Cajun chicken salad with creamy Cajun dressing, and homemade crab sandwiches. Those homemade crab sandwiches are excellent if I do say so myself. And for dessert my very own version of French Quarter Beignet with fresh sweet strawberries."

Eris studied her dish of Gator Gumbo in silence and watched to see what Camille would do.

Tiara grabbed her spoon and dug in, not wasting any time. "Mmmm, this is scrumptious."

"This does look appetizing," Camille said, picking up her spoon and taking up a spoon full of Gator Gumbo. She blew on it to cool it down and then took a bite. "Mmmm! Oh, my goodness this is tasty!" She said filling her spoon again and having another bite.

Quickly Eris followed Camille's lead. "Oh, my goodness! This is some incredible stuff!"

A half hour later, "I think it's time we tell you why we are here," Camille stated.

Grand-mere Catherine exhaled. "Trouble following you three like a bad storm. I can feel it. Well, you know what I say, don't trouble with trouble, until trouble troubles with you."

"Try saying that one ten times," Eris giggled.

Tiara tried to snuff out her laughter. "I don't mean to laugh. But everyone looks so serious," she sighed. "But Grand-mere Catherine, I'm the one this is affecting, and I suspect I might not be dealing with something from this earth. If you get my understanding?"

Grand-mere Catherine turned and focus on Tiara. She nodded. "Well Tiara, that doesn't sound strange to me. At least I can see you've got a firm understanding that sometimes in life we ain't always dealing with the living. Things ain't always what they seem on this earth."

Tiara sat back in her chair with a worried look on her face.

She sighed heavily. She began to realize the few chances she had in life to just spend quality time, like the time she was having right now with her best friends and this kind, gentle wise woman. It made her realize what was really important in life. And then her thoughts shifted to Delmar, and all the strange things that kept happening. Taking time out to look at things differently made her remember why she'd come. She cleared her throat. "Grand-mere Catherine? Have you ever heard of someone being able to change into another person?"

There was a strange kind of quiet.

Grand-mere Catherine examined Tiara's face. She took her time doing so. "Let me see you hand child."

Suddenly she took Tiara's hand in hers and scrutinized her palm slowly. After a short time, she leaned back in her chair and looked off into the distance for a moment and then exhaled slowly. "Lord have mercy, Tiara, something has happened to you."

She turned and looked at Camille and Eris. "Now you two tell me exactly what you saw, when you thought you saw your friend Tiara, that night," she said bluntly.

Puzzled Tiara asked. "They told you about that?"

Grand-mere Catherine glanced at Tiara as if she was speaking Martian. "Evidently they didn't tell me the whole truth and Lord knows I hate liars."

Abruptly Tiara stood and walked around the spacious kitchen, as if in deep reflection.

Camille and Eris looked at each other and started talking at once. "We never told you we saw Tiara, just that we saw someone we thought was Tiara."

"Yeah, Camille's right," Eris, affirmed. "We saw someone who looked like Tiara and she was wearing her favorite dress, but she wasn't acting like Tiara normally acts."

"Okay, now we're getting someplace," Grand-mere Catherine declared, bluntly. "Now, tell me the whole story."

Slowly Camille and Eris told Grand-mere Catherine what they saw that night.

When they finished. Grand-mere Catherine turned and glanced across the room at Tiara. "Tiara," she said in a gentle voice, "I have to ask you, do you remember who you were with. I mean besides Zack."

Tiara walked back to the table and sat down. She put her head in her hands. "I remember telling Zack I was going to the lady's room," she shivered. "I saw Diademe when I was going into the lady's room."

Grand-mere Catherine raised one quivering eyebrow and said the name softly. "Diademe…"

"Who's Diademe?" Eris asked.

"Oh, I remember your saying something about a lady named Diademe, when I picked you up that morning from the Fairmont Hotel, Tiara," Camille remarked. "Strange though I never got a chance to meet her."

"How terribly odd," Grand-mere Catherine remarked. "Tiara did you know that your name means a headband made of rich decoration, worn by those to show a sign of royalty?"

"My mom sometimes mentioned it," Tiara said.

Grand-mere Catherine nodded. "Did you also know that Diademe is the French for Tiara?"

Tiara shivered. "No! I didn't know that."

Eris nudged Camille with her elbow. "This is beginning to sound like some twisted, weird spooky shhhhh --!"

Grand-mere Catherine blurted. "Eris Simeon! I do not allow curse words in my home," she replied, and added a soft smile. "Now of course, if I'm using them, its different story."

"Give me your hands, Tiara," Grand-mere Catherine commanded and then tilted her head concentrating as if gauging something like she was clairvoyant.

Eris leaned in close to Camille and whispered. "Is it true that old woman is psychic?"

"Hush!" Camille blurted.

It seemed like a full minute passed before Grand-mere Catherine broke her concentration and turned and looked back at Tiara.

The suspense in the room increased.

Then Grand-mere Catherine paused as if she was listening to someone and then she stared off into the distance as if she was seeing something. And then she sees it. Something chasing Tiara, always hiding in the dark. A shadowy shape with different colored eyes. *What color are they?* She wondered trying to get a better look. Green, the eyes were green. The strangest green she'd ever seen. Vivid like the green on the feathers of a Peacock. The dark shapeshifts, moves silently like the wind. slowly the dark form took shape. The shape became a woman's body. Long black hair blew in the wind and covered the face. A voice picked up on the wind and bellowed out in a tremendous wail. *He wounded me! He broke my heart!* It was a woman's sad voice. *You only get one love in a lifetime! He was mine! He was mine!* Something was familiar, the woman's form had a family resemblance.

Through her blurred tunnel vision, Grand-mere Catherine tried to see clearly the woman's face but her long flowing air covered it. All at once she sensed danger. Hands pulling a body down through black water. She could feel the resentment, the hatred, the anger. She could sense something else too. The dark woman's form was strong. It was powerful. It was bitter. Something bad was about to happen. She felt the panic.

Tiara could sense it too. All at once she jerked her hands out of Grand-mere Catherine. "Oh, my goodness! Something bad is going to happen!"

"Oh, Christ!" Eris shrilled out. "We need Jesus."

"What happened? What did you see?" Camille taut voice permeated the air.

The three friends all began talking at once.

"Enough!" Grand-mere Catherine bellowed. "You should learn not to assume everything you think you see in a vision is real."

She took a deep breath. "Ladies, you all must remain calm. There is something going on here. Something to do with ghosts. But I have a strong feeling something else is going on here too. I smelled a strong floral scent as well as another scent. It was stronger," Grand-mere Catherine stated.

Camille cleared her throat. "So, what are you going to do to help Tiara?"

Puzzled Grand-mere Catherine glanced at her. "What kind of help?"

"I mean to protect Tiara?" Camille replied. "You know give her a talisman or something? Put a protective spell around her."

Grand-mere Catherine shook her head. "No. But I am going to look into it. I have a lot of unanswered questioned. But I don't think any of you can give me answers and a talisman won't do any good."

"Why not?" The three friends asked together.

Grand-mere Catherine slowly gave them a smile. "Don't you know? Can't you feel it. Some powerful woman has already put a protective spell around Tiara."

All at once Grand-mere Catherine enfolded Tiara in an embrace and then cupping her hands at either sides of Tiara's head and then running then down the sides of her body. She then abruptly stopped stepped back and looked at her.

Tiara shrugged embarrassed. For a moment she was too shocked to move. "What was that for? I don't understand."

All at once, Grand-mere Catherine exhaled grabbed Tiara's hand and patted it. "It's just as I thought."

"What are you talking about?" Tiara asked, her expression bewildered. "I don't understand."

Grand-mere Catherine stared hard into Tiara's eyes. "We don't have much time."

"Time for what?"

A frown wrinkled Grand-mere Catherine's brow. "Time for your training," she answered, sternly. "You will have to do battle soon with forces not of this world."

Chapter 21

Grand-mere Catherine, Bingo Queen, Glenda & Consuelo

Glenda sashayed to the window and checked for the arrival of her guests again, Consuelo spread the ancient-looking book down and chated. "Now Glenda, who is this Mrs. Catherine Marie Rousseau-La Cour?"

"You recall her Consuelo, she's Delta Dawn Allemande sister."

Consuelo wandered over and fetched a brownie. "Oh, those Cane River Louisiana Creole sisters? Yes, of course. But I didn't recognize her by her complete name, Mrs. Catherine Marie Rousseau-Andries La Cour, no indeed, merely by Grand-mere ..."

"They fondly call her Grand-mere Catherine," Glenda replied deliberately cutting her off. "I guess everyone around knows her by that nickname. She should be here soon with her great friend Gabby Baptiste."

"Now I do recall Gabby Baptiste is the Bingo Queen, I see her often enough at Aqua Maids Bingo Hall," Consuelo snickered. "She's a lot of fun. But I don't think she's clairvoyant."

"No, but Catherine Marie Rousseau-Andries La Cour is," Glenda replied.

Consuelo shook her head. "So, is her sister, Delta Dawn Allemande," she answered with a heavy Spanish accent. "Something to do with their Cane River Louisiana Creole roots. I think Nona, knows them."

The buzzer rang out loud just as Consuelo finished talking.

"Sounds like our guests have arrived," she suggested watching Glenda head for the front door.

Glenda paused at the door to her home and felt for a

vibration. She wanted to gauge a tremor of any suspicious energy before she opened the front door. Feeling nothing out of the ordinary she quickly opened the door.

"Come on in ladies," Glenda cheerfully announced.

Grand-mere Catherine quickly walked in followed by Gabby Baptiste.

"Hello Glenda, thanks for letting us drop by for a visit," Grand-mere Catherine countered. "You remember my good friend Gabby Baptiste?"

Gabby strolled over and stood in front of Glenda. "Of course, you recognize me, Glenda," she giggled. "Haven't seen you at Bingo in a few years."

Glenda frowned I was hoping you'd forget seeing we there, all-together. I haven't admitted it to Consuelo yet, that Bingo used to be my passion."

Gabby paused, "Consuelo ain't gonna hold that against you and neither am I. Hell, I'm proud of my Bingo obsession. Hell, if Bingo was a man, I'd be shouting to the world I'm addicted to me some him," she whooped.

Gabby walked further into the room. "Where is Consuelo?"

"Hey, Gabby, and Grand-mere Catherine," Consuelo called, with a heavy Spanish accent. "I'm over here," she answered, reaching for another brownie. "Thought I'd try to hurry and eat up the brownies and help keep you both from putting any weight on those slim figures of yours. I swear you two never gain a pound."

Gabby grinned and strolled over. "Hmmm," she replied picking up a brownie from under plastic cover. "Those sure look delicious. Since I'm a guest, I don't mind if I help myself. You realize we are famished after that long car ride from San Jose to San Juan Baptista."

Grand-mere Catherine patted Gabby's hand. "Gabby my dear, I must love you like a family member because I swear you ain't never had a single lesson in good old fashion Southern home training. Mind your manners and save some of those brownies for me," she snickered.

"Would you look at this spread." Gabby exclaimed.

Glenda joined them. "You know I do have some Southern home training and there was no way I wasn't going to layout a spread of food for my friends to enjoy."

An hour later, the teakettle whistled and chirped as Glenda poured it over a teapot filled with tea leaves. She took it back to the table and placed an over a cup and poured. She gently poured four cups of tea, and then cautiously lifted a cup and saucer and placed it in front of her and poured.

Sitting the teapot back in front of her she said. "Okay, Grand-mere Catherine tell me the reason for your visit?"

"Hold your horses," Gabby muttered, "My tea still piping hot. Now, pass me that tray of tea cookies, so I can dip my tea cookie in and sip. Then yawl can talk."

Grand-mere Catherine shook her head and glanced at Gabby as she passed the tea cookies. "Now, that we have Gabby quiet, I'll tell you why I made the drive down to see you privately," she raised a brow as she turned toward Glenda. "I suspect you are aware we have a visitor from another, shall we say dimension? That I believe you two ladies are already know about."

Glenda shook her head back and forth. "Surely, I can't even imagine what you're talking about."

Grand-mere Catherine took a deep breath. "Remember who you are speaking too." She kept her voice as level as she could. "All I want to know is if she is a demon?"

Glenda had been afraid of this. She knew Grand-mere Catherine knew something, and she knew that it was a woman. She wondered how. She stared back at Grand-mere Catherine hard. "How did you know it's a woman?"

"It's a woman, for real?" Gabby added, dipping another tea cookie into her tea and taking a bite. "Grand-mere Catherine you never told me it was a woman. Hell, you never told me much about it, to begin with. Now, I've got to worry about an evil ass third dimension demon-woman running around loose and fast in San Jose."

"Gabby, she may not be from the third dimension," Grand-mere Catherine said. "Many dimensions exist to separate the realms."

"Yes, they do," Consuelo added with traces of her Spanish

accent. "I have a great love for studying the
complex levels of consciousness and the most extreme experience of
separation in both the physical and non-physical world. Did you
know that there are five levels of the soul, or consciousness,
corresponding to the various planes of reality?"

Gabby shook her head. "Nope, I hadn't a clue and I can
honestly say it never interested me enough to look for a clue."

Consuelo laughed. "Oh, now that was funny! That's why I
love being around you Gabby you are always so much fun."

"Would you look at this spread?" Gabby said. "Who fixed
up all of this?

"Mostly it was Glenda," Consuelo said. "She did a fine job!"

"Yes, I think so," Gabby declared. "I'm enjoying these cute
little sandwiches and the fresh muffins. Not to mention I think I'll
need a couple of the recipes. For my daughter, Camille, of course. I
ain't into the cooking thing anymore like I used to be."

Grand-mere Catherine patted her forehead. She'd been
afraid of this. Gabby was good for getting folks off the subject. Now
she'd have to get them back on subject. "Gabby, please. We'll talk
recipes later. We need to stay focus. This is serious."

"Here! Here!" Consuelo interjected. "Yes, of course we must
stay focus," she said, tilting her head and giving Grand-mere
 Catherine her undivided attention. "Do you suppose we are dealing
with a *huli jing?"*

"What is a *huli jing*?" Gabby inquired

It's an ancient mythical creature," Consuelo replied.

"Every culture has a different legend attached to it. In
Chinese mythology, its says it is an animal like a fox who
can transform itself into a beautiful woman or a male and if it
becomes a human it can have sexual relations with members of the
opposite sex," Grand-mere Catherine added.

Glenda nodded agreement. "I heard it said that it has great
powers to know things. It can know things thousands of miles a way
and it can bewilder even the wisest man or woman and poison their
minds and possess them."

Grand-mere Catherine nodded agreement. "There are many
things to consider about what it could be. It's possible even that it
could be we have is a shapeshifting spirit. But it could also be a soul

walking around without a body."

"If it is, then, we got a way bigger problem," Glenda interrupted.

"Look God is the creator of everything!" Gabby stated, feeling the need to add her two cents worth. "Yawl better get back to church on Sunday and tell the Creator who engineered the heaven and the earth he has a problem."

"It doesn't work like that Gabby," Grand-mere Catherine explained. "You see, God gave us all free will. She's already loose. She's here on this earth, on her own free will, and we've got to figure out how to make her go back."

"You sure do seem to know a lot of about this lost soul," Gabby said. "In fact, this is the first time I've heard you go into such details. Does this lady soul, have a name?" Gabby inquired.

With a sense of utter dread, Grand-mere Catherine glanced at the faces staring at her across the table.

Glenda leaned forward. "You know something, I can tell. You've met her? Right?" She asked cocking her head to one side.

Consuelo flashed her a bright smile. "Tell us, have you? You have? Haven't you, Grand-mere Catherine?"

Grand-mere Catherine leaned in close and glance between Glenda and Consuelo face before she nodded an affirmative. "Okay, but, first you tell me how this lost soul found her way to this earth and then I'll share what I know, fair enough?"

"Done," Glenda said, waving her hand.

Consuelo agreed.

Glenda leaned back in her chair and blinked rapidly. "This all started when Delmar Deveraux paid, Nona, Consuelo and myself a visit," she replied, filling in the story and then finally declaring. "The next thing I know, I'm here at the bar with my husband, Scott Irishman-Jackson and we get a visit from Common and Fannie," she said telling them the rest of the story.

"Huh! Huh! Huh!" Gabby murmured loudly. "Nothing ever good comes from meeting with Common, Fannie and the Devil! Even I know that."

Consuelo crossed herself. "I believe you are right, my friend. But it was only Common and Fannie."

Grand-mere Catherine and Gabby glance at each other, with

dubious expressions on their faces.

"You can bet the devil walked through the door with those two. Seen or unseen," Grand-mere Catherine added. "I've learned that much since I have been living this long."

"I had a strange feeling something else was present in the room, while Common and Fannie were visiting," Glenda spoke out.

"You'd been better off having a meeting with Papa Legba at the crossroads," Grand-mere Catherine replied. "At least he'd have enough common sense to make sure any portals, he used to come through, were closed, properly."

"This is some hilarious, shit," Gabby chortled. "If I do say so myself and I ain't into all that magic hocus pocus stuff like you ladies are."

Grand-mere Catherine turned and looked at Glenda. "So, let me get this straight. Common and Fannie, paid you a visit, right? They used a travel portal, right?"

Glenda cleared her throat. "It's partially right. They paid a visit and then we had another visitor who used the travel portal. That visitor was an ancestor of Delmar Devereaux. He told us about the curse that began when he lived and had a relationship with a lady love who is the ancestor..."

"Of, Tiara Blake," Grand-mere Catherine interrupted and finished her sentence. "Of course, this all makes sense."

"Okay, fill us in." Glenda demanded.

Grand-mere Catherine took a deep breath. "Well, I had a visit from Tiara Blake, and her two best friends, Camille Baptiste and Eris Simeon. It seems Camille and Eris had witnessed something strange one night," she said, telling them the story.

Glenda let out a deep sigh. "Wow! What a story. I'm trying to wrap my mind around all of it."

Grand-mere Catherine let out a sigh longer than Glenda. "I left out one thing. The woman that Camille and Eris saw has a name," she looked back at the faces staring back at her. "Her name is Diademe."

Glenda shivered. "And Diademe is the French word for Tiara."

Consuelo grimaced. "Is it possible we are dealing with the woman Delmar's ancestor wronged during his lifetime on earth?"

"That would be easy to deal with," Glenda said. "I suspect we are dealing with something entirely different and I think Grand-mere Catherine agrees."

"What?" Gabby excitingly asked.

Glenda and Grand-mere Catherine eyes met. A long moment passed.

"Well?" Consuelo shrugged, as she glanced between Glenda and Grand-mere Catherine. "How much longer are you two going to keep us in suspense?"

 Say what are you two doing staring at each other like that?" Gabby asked. "Trying to read each others minds?"

"I can read plenty of minds if I wanted to," Glenda said. "But now is not the time."

"But not mine," Grand-mere Catherine replied. "Yet I do know what you are thinking."

Grand-mere Catherine turned her attention to Consuelo and Gabby. "You see ladies, a scorn woman has been found throughout history and she can wreak some of the worst havoc ever known to mankind."

Glenda nodded. "I see your point hell has no fury like a woman scorned. What we are dealing with here is a woman who was rejected in love. So, it isn't Tiara's ancestor who came through the portal when Delmar's ancestor crossed through the portal. We were only told the story of how Delmar's ancestor raped the woman he loved to force her to marry him."

"Only, she committed suicide taking their unborn baby with her," Consuelo added.

"Therefore, Tiara's ancestor never came through the travel portal because she killed herself to get away from Delmar," Gabby stated.

"You almost have it right, only Tiara's ancestor didn't kill herself. She didn't commit suicide. Don't you see? This, story is as old as time," Grand-mere Catherine interjected.

"What?" Gabby said. "I missed something in translation. How is this story as old as time! And what happened to Tiara's ancestor?"

"She was murdered," Glenda whispered.

Suddenly tiny notes of music rang out from a piano sitting

off in the corner.

All heads turned toward the piano.

The music played. As a shrill silvery eerie voice sang out.

Is it my love?

Where forth art thou my love?

Ask me again that question...

Where forth art thou my love?

Is it my love?

Speak to me my love

Speak to me my love in your soft voice

And whisper to me again that you love me

Look into my eyes

I am looking into your eyes

Do you see me?

Let me see you

Oh, please see me

Please don't make me sad and blue

Love me... Love me

Oh, please love me

Will thou believe so kindly of my fault

For my fault is my passion for you

I call my love passion

You call my love madness

When you say you do not want me?

I cringe in despair

I can not bare

That you do not care

Oh, can you not hear?

Each tear I shed is for you my dear

You did not understand my foolishness.

Can you not guess my madness?

My madness is my passion

For I have loved only you.

Where are you my love?

My one love in a lifetime…

I need you back in my life…

Please come back to me my love…

You only get one love in a lifetime…

The shrill silvery eerie voice tapered off.

And then a loud thunderous raucous voice echoed. "I shed no tears for no man! I am she! I am not the evil one! I am the wronged one. But there is an evil one! There is …"

The voice trailed off into a whisper and disappeared right before the piano stopped playing.

A ghastly sound blasted out singing like rushing reeds and suddenly all voices ceased.

"Damn! Damn! Damn!" Gabby said jumping up. "I get so sick and tired of this Wizard of the Oz wicked witch bullshit! I'm ready to get the hell out of here now. And I ain't talking about going to the land of Oz!"

Glenda, unfazed by the whole scene. "Well, looks like we are working with good and evil."

"Yes, we are," Grand-mere Catherine interjected, glancing around the room. "Did you see that image in the mirror when the scared ghost was singing?"

"It was a demon," Consuelo said. "Looking for a host."

"A host?" Gabby asked.

Glenda shrugged. "No need to be concerned about it."

"All hell! How can you say that?" Gabby asked, sounding shocked.

"She can say that because it's true. It's after something but nothing connected to us," Grand-mere Catherine. *"At least nothing I'm going to share here tonight,"* she thought to herself.

As if reading her thoughts, Glenda's eyes locked with Grand-mere Catherine and they acknowledged a mutual understanding.

"You know Gabby you are right, it's time we headed home to San Jose," Grand-mere Catherine suggested. "Why don't you go and help Consuelo get started clearing up. Glenda and I will be in shortly to help the two of you. The sooner we finish the quicker we can leave."

She waited as Gabby and Consuelo took several dishes to the kitchen.

Once they were out of the room she and Glenda headed for a private spot.

"Glenda, what are you going to do?" She asked but didn't wait for a response. "May I suggest that you increase your protection spell on Delmar, and Tiara."

"I couldn't agree with you more," Glenda replied.

Chapter 22
Queen Calafia

Delmar couldn't believe the hang-over he had for the last couple of days. Because of the pain it gave him, he never left town to go back to his home by Monterey Bay.

He put on his dark shades and headed out the front door of his residence in downtown San Jose. Just as he did Nona was stepping out of the elevator.

"Good evening Delmar, are you ready to go and see the Queen?"

Delmar rubbed his jaw. "Has it been seven days already?" he inquired.

"Yes, it has, and it is time we took off for our journey," Nona replied. "Take a look at the map," she said taking the high-quality parchment paper scroll from a hidden pocket."

The parchment paper was a map vividly and distinctively showing all the places they had travel on their *Quest*.

"Wow!" Delmar exclaimed. "The map shows we are at the end of our *Quest*. This is the last item we need."

"Yes! It is Delmar! We are almost done," Nona declared. "By the way, I have something for you."

"For me? What is it?" Delmar eagerly inquired.

Nona reached into her pocket and pulled out a necklace. "Here let me put this around your neck. It's a talisman. Never take it off. It will protect you. One day, it might even save your life. If something surreal happens while we are on this journey grab your talisman for protection."

Nona spoke a silent prayer inside her mind she knew that talismans have been used since the dawn of mankind to enhance fertility, ward off evil and bring luck. She prayed it would keep Delmar safe where they were going.

Delmar waited while Nona placed the necklace around his neck before he inquired where they were headed as they entered the elevator.

"So how are we traveling this time?"

Nona was caught up in the prayer inside her mind. Silently in her mind, she kept chanting the prayer over and over again.

When she didn't say a word, he asked again. "So where do we go to find our travel portal? You realize, since we have been traveling by this method, I've become fascinated with time travel."

At the sound of the passion in Delmar's voice, Nona woke out of her trance and giggled "You do sound enthuse," she answered laughing. "It is a fascinating topic, time traversal."

"Yes, it is a fascinating subject," Delmar replied. "I've picked up several books on the subject and so far, I have not been disappointed."

The elevator door closed behind them. "This elevator seems like the ideal travel portal to me," Nona replied.

Delmar glanced at her. As their eyes met, he knew exactly what was about to happen when she pushed the closed-door button.

"Don't you just love magical powers of transportation, Delmar," Nona asked as their portkey of transport took them out into the unknown.

The next thing Delmar knew he was standing in front of a large massive entrance that resembled a Skull. He knew immediately it had to be the entrance of Pluto's cave at Mount Shasta. He shifted and looked back, and he saw the gigantic mountains range of Mount Shasta looming in the distance.

Nona nudged him, and he turned back around and followed her into the entrance.

Pluto's Cave was formed by an eruption of a basaltic lava and was believed to be roughly 190,000-year-old. The cave was a collapsed lava tube and got its name after the Greek God of the Underworld.

Delmar abruptly stopped walking and glanced around. There were lava beds as far as the eye could see. He gauged that they had been walking for almost an hour. "How much further?"

"Hopefully, not much," Nona said, pausing to take a breath. "We're looking for the mythical entrance, it is believed to be the entrance to the ancient city of "City of Eternal Sunshine" also called Coachella."

"No kidding?" Delmar asked amazed and fascinated by Nona's knowledge. What else do you know?"

"Well, the California public school system has a history class that teaches that Pluto's cave was believed to be an inner-Earth gateway entrance along activated key line meridians on the northern side of Mount Shasta," Nona replied. "Did you know that the Native Americans around these parts has known about this for years? And they tell that there are pyramidic buttes and etheric temples that hold mysterious energies. Pluto's Cave is an ideal place for a vision quest, you know."

"A vision quest, seriously?" Delmar asked looking bewildered.

"Don't look so skeptical, Delmar. Legend has it that from the moment we stepped through the entrance a spirit guardian has been watching us the whole time. And if we are lucky, we might just get to experience the vortex."

"Wow, you know I heard vortex paranormal portals can sometimes act as the doorway to the afterlife?" he asked.

"You got it," Nona assured him.

"Fascinating, I can hardly wait," Delmar declared sarcastically.

Suddenly as if on cue, the temperature in the cave changed dramatically. A positive upward flow of energy seemed to shoot up from the earth as a cloudy fog of murky vapor rose out of nowhere.

"Do you feel that Delmar?" Nona asked but didn't wait for a reply. "That energy power you feel right now is balanced, that's the yin and yang balance."

Delmar knew he was standing there grinning. He felt the vortex alright. He'd never felt so much bliss, love, joy excitement at one time. "I feel so happy."

"That's good," Nona said. "It means you're having a good experience in the vortex. It shouldn't be long now, I think we are on our way to see the Queen."

Instantly, divine light showed itself like a golden halo around the sun on the wall of the cave. A massive tunnel popped up out of nowhere and held a golden door that slowly opened. Rays of light beckon them to enter.

Nona looked at Delmar and spoke without speaking. *"Come,*

follow me."

Delmar stepped slowly through the doorway into another world. He adjusted his eyes and heard the soothing sounds of rushing water. He took a deep breath and thought the air that he breathed in was the sweetest, and freshest air he'd ever smelled.

The valley before him was breathtaking, unlike anything he'd ever seen. It's mesmerizing landscape so magical you couldn't wrap your mind around how a barren desert coexisted with a rich fertile bio-diverse oasis. Lush with wild plants, date palm trees, and abundant forests.

Delmar gasped. "This is hard to comprehend. A world that time has forgotten."

Nona tilted her head listening. "Do you hear that?"

Delmar shook his head. "No." But looking out over the valley floor below. He saw the trees in the forest swaying and moving. Something was coming.

"Look!" Nona pointed.

Delmar looked where she was pointing. Something was coming. He saw the fire, but it wasn't spreading to anything even though a soft wind was blowing. He instantly knew the fire was a blazing torch in the distance.

He heard the pounding of hooves before he saw the horses. "Look, warriors. I don't believe it. It's like time has stopped."

"Do you notice anything about the warriors, Delmar?" Nona asked.

Delmar looked closer. The riders were only a short distance away. But he noticed their breast armor. "Oh shit! Their women!"

Nona snickered. "That's why I enjoy traveling with you Delmar you are so insightful."

The women warriors drew their horses in front of them. The two women in the front were each pulling an extra horse.

The women warrior's golden bronze bodies were magnificently strong, lean, robust and toned. Rich vivid gold and turquoise, tourmaline and garnet stoned necklaces hung around their necks and wrist.

"Greetings, I am Siachen, and this is Cree we are the warrior daughters of Queen Calafia. We were sent to welcome you."

"Greetings Siachen and Cree, I am Nona, and this is

Delmar."

Siachen did all the talking. "Come, we have horses for you to ride. We must go. Queen Calafia is waiting for you, back at the fortress."

Nona and Delmar mounted their horses.

Siachen led the way. They rode through the thick dark forest, the torches lighting the way.

A luminous moon glowed brilliantly against a vivid deep blue night sky as silvery clouds soared high. There was a calming breeze of a night wind all around them as they traveled.

Soon, a magnificent mountain loomed in front of them. "Our cliff rock palace- fortress, is perched high on the mountain rocks above," Siachen pointed out, as she brought in their horses to a slow trot as they reached a gigantic stone.

Delmar glanced up and saw hundreds of torched flames giving light and warmth as they cascaded down the side of the mountain.

Siachen's voice song out in a high-pitched sound alerting that she had arrived.

Instantly the gigantic stone rolled a way and Siachen entered.

Cree waved her hand beckoning Delmar and Nona to follow behind Siachen as she took up the rear as they all entered through the massive entryway.

A guard met them inside and helped Nona off her horse.

"Nona," Delmar whispered softly. "Do you see this place?"

An old woman brought over a tray of water and put it down on a table beside them. "Water?" she inquired.

"Yes, I'm parched," Delmar answered, watching as she poured him a cup.

Smiling, as he lifted his cup. "Bottoms up," he said, taking a swallow.

The water tasted sweet.

"Mmmm, this is so refreshing. Like no water I've ever tasted," Delmar said.

Nona joined him and asked for a drink.

The elderly woman poured her a cup.

Nona raised her cup to Delmar. "To our quest."

"And to our friendship, my good friend Nona, I could never

have made it here without you," Delmar replied.

Nona took a sip of her drink and Delmar joined her.

They quickly downed the cool refreshing water.

Cree looked at them smiling. "Come we must go, Siachen has gone ahead to let Queen Calafia know we are coming," she waved her hand. "Come I will show you the way."

A few minutes later, they walked into the palace courtyard. An exuberant welcome awaited them. Sitting high above a long, long table sat Queen Calafia, in all her royal splendor. She was dressed in a vibrate red dress with a chunky solid gold necklace statement collar that held a perfect looking large pear shaped stone in the center. The stone was a snow white quarts with veins of pure gold running through it. A Sheer gold shimmer long scarf draped behind her.

"Come closer," Queen Calafia commanded.

Delmar slowly approached her. By God, she was the most beautiful woman he had ever seen. But there was more. She looked familiar. "Who are you? I mean you look like someone…"

Queen Calafia interrupted him and bellowed. "I am yesterday, today and tomorrow. I am sorrow, hope and dreams unfulfilled. I am she who knows all. She who knows your fate."

Queen Calafia, she rose and placed her hand on his shoulder. "Welcome, my friend. Please take your seat down there Delmar, by Siachen and Cree. They know why you have come and where you need to go," she said, dismissing him. "I wish Nona to sit by me."

Nona looked puzzled. "Delmar and I have…"

"I know what you have need of Nona, remember I am Queen Calafia," she said. "It is important that you and I talk and besides Siachen and Cree, will be taking Delmar away shortly."

Queen Calafia turned her attention and looked around the room. As if not finding what she was looking for her voice rang out. "Rattlesnake!"

A giant Amazon woman walked into the room. "Yes, my Queen?"

"Have some food brought out for our guest, and bring me some cactus wine," Queen Calafia said.

Instantly an elderly woman brought over a tray of with a

beautifully carved gold pitcher and cups. She poured the Queen's cup and placed it in front of her. She then turned and did the same for Nona.

Trays of food loaded with fruits, chicken, pork, and beef was placed in front of them. The aroma made Nona's stomach growl.

"Help yourself, Nona," Queen Calafia said.

Nona did as she was told and grabbed herself a roast chicken leg. She took a bite and closed her eyes. The flavor was intoxicating. She washed down her chicken with the cactus wine. Before she knew it her cup was empty.

"You like cactus wine, I see," Queen Calafia said.

"Yes, it looks like I do," Nona replied.

No worries, there is more."

"Queen Calafia might I inquire about the white stone in your necklace. I've never seen anything like it."

"You have excellent taste this stone we call gold snow, the viens of gold running through it are real gold. It is the stone of my people," Queen Calafia said.

Just then Rattlesnake moved in close and refilled the Queen's cactus wine. She then turned and refilled the cup in front of Nona.

Queen Calafia took a sip of her cactus wine and then said. "I'm afraid we have a problem, Nona."

"Oh?" Nona replied, swallowing a bite of her chicken.

"Yes," the Queen went on.

Queen Calafia waved her hand. "Rattlesnake, bring the crystal, please."

Rattlesnake walked over and retrieved a coiled twined lidded basket in colors of white, brown and red. She planted the basket in front of Nona, removed the lid making sure she placed it directly in front of Nona. Then she picked up the basket and gradually, poured Crystal Rose Quartz stones into the lid.

Nona took her free hand reached over and picked up a hand full of Crystal Rose quartz stones and let them slide through her fingers. "I don't see the problem. There is more than enough Rose Quartz here."

"The Rose Quartz is not the problem," Queen Calafia said. "Do you believe in fate Nona?"

Nona looked at the chicken leg in her one hand and the Rose

quartz stones in the other. She made a mistake. She looked down at the table where Delmar should have been sitting. He was gone. She had a problem. A big problem.

"Where's Delmar," Nona demanded.

"Why? What is he to you?" Queen Calafia asked.

Nona couldn't swallow. She was distraught. She had no idea where Delmar could be in this place. "He's... Well, he's nothing to me. It's just that I feel responsible for him," she countered.

Queen Calafia sighed heavily. "That shows you have a good heart," she paused. "Still, you did not answer my question?"

Nona considered the eyes of Queen Calafia and saw something powerful and fierce. Wisdom shone back at her like a great knowing. Except something was off. Nona couldn't put her finger on it. But something was wrong here.

Nona let out a deep sigh and said. "Sometimes we believe things are meant to be, sometimes when life doesn't go our way, or we cannot make sense of an event or outcome, we believe fate is happening to us."

"I see you have doubt." Queen Calafia said.

"I believe you can fight your fate," Nona said. "Under certain circumstances."

Queen Calafia laughed. "You cannot fight fate."

"If your love is powerful! If your love is true! You can fight fate and you can win," Nona declared.

Queen Calafia laughed. "Interesting, have you seen this done?"

Nona gave Queen Calafia a fierce look. She reached into her pocket to find her talisman. She needed all the power that it possessed. Frantically she began rubbing it as she mentally began saying a powerful enchantment in her mind. She focused her mind. She needed to tune in to the oneness the invisible side of life. She said a strong prayer that Delmar could hear her. She prayed that he could be in oneness with her.

Loudly she cleared her throat determine to make sure Queen Calafia saw her eyes. "Yes, Queen Calafia, I have seen it done. I have seen fate defeated by love. For Love is the most powerful energy God has ever made!"

Queen Calafia laughter filled the courtyard.

***

Elsewhere in the palace-fortress, Delmar couldn't understand how he had found his way to this room. He wondered if the cactus wine he had been drinking was spiked.

He tried to rise and realized he was lying on a bed of pillows. His head was throbbing. He wanted to get out of there before he heard that voice again. And then the voice came.

A woman was singing in an eerie disembodied voice that melted coldly around the room.

"You loved me… You loved me… I gave you my heart Delmar!

He heard wolves howling in the distance. He opened his eyes and looked at the ceiling. He thought he saw footsteps leaving the imprint on the ceiling.

Delmar just laid there staring at the ceiling and suddenly he heard footsteps soft like a woman's. With a groan, he tried to get up.

A woman cackled. He felt a grip on his shoulder. He glanced over his shoulder and noticed nothing was there. He felt the shoved as something forced him backward against the pillows.

"Uh Huh! No, you don't Delmar, no fleeing. You are all mine to do as I please," the woman's ghostly cry rung out. "Just as I was once all yours."

Delmar thought that he was losing his mind. The woman's voice sounded familiar. Someone from his past. Some how he knew it wasn't in this lifetime. It was from a past existence.

"Take me back to Nona, please," he mumbled incoherently.

Pictures flashed before his eyes. A jumble of images flashed before his eyes. A woman, a baby, a shovel and then the hang man's rope. And then he felt pain, and anguish. And then the terror as he stood before the open grave. Somebody wanted him dead. He knew it. He felt it deep inside.

He squeezed his eyes tighter, there had to me more. There had to be. Where was the love. He had to feel the love. He rummaged through his memories until he found what he was looking for.

The punch to his face came out of nowhere. The pain was so excruciating, Delmar yelled out. "What the hell is happening?"

"I'm going to make you pay for not wanting me!" The woman's voice bellowed, like death on the wind.

Delmar took the next blow and howled when he felt the blood run out of his nose.

"I will never let you leave me, Delmar! Never!" she yelled.

Delmar listened to the sound of her voice and gauge how close she was to him in the darkened room.

He thought long and hard and decided he needed to buy himself some time while he figured out what to do. He spoke the first thing that came to his mind. "Hey, ghost!" He yelled. "I have no idea of what you heard about me. But what I do know is that that evil can hide in plain sight. Are you an evil spirit?" Delmar asked but didn't wait for a response. " I have heard that an evil spirit can bewilder man or woman and make them powerless."

The ghost of a woman laughter crackled out. "You have heard right!"

For several minutes Delmar sat and listen to the ghostly woman's eerie disembodied voice sing out cold laughter around the room. He grimaced feeling the insanity eating at his emotions. He thought all was lost as his hands cupped his face. He clamped his ears tight before letting his hands cascade down the side of his face to his neck. His fingertips caressed the talisman. He felt the force of power ignite and surge through his mind.

"Nona! Help me!" Delmar screamed in his mind.

"Delmar you cannot show mercy to evil, or you will become a pawn in their game. Steel yourself! You have the power!" Nona's voice rung out through his mind.

With a deep knowing, Delmar felt his body illuminate with the spirit of a power greater than him.

Quietly and carefully he took his time and measured the distance between them in his mind.

When he knew exactly how far she was from him he leaped forward with a force so fierce it even surprised him when he rushed his body into a headlong ram.

"Ouch! Damn! Damn! Damn! My head is bleeding! What kind of power do you possess? How did you do that? My head is bleeding!" The woman moaned, as her voice trembled.

He pulled back to get a good look at her face. "It's you!

I thought you were a ghost," Delmar said, with his face closed to hers. "I thought ghosts weren't supposed to feel pain."

He thought for a moment. "You look like my Tiara, but I know you are not, Tiara. You maybe a ghost from my ancestor's past. I don't know what you're doing in my world. But I want you gone!"

As if Delmar had commanded her. The ghost woman emited cracking sucking sounds before a deep chill filled the air and it floated gradually toward the stone floor.

Delmar stood and watched the ghost form fold like a heap to the floor.

"I don't know what kind of sick twisted game this is, but I'm out of here," he said, as he continued to talk to himself looking for the door.

He barely stepped through the door when he looked back at the misty vapor on the floor. "It looks like you came from hell expecting to take me back with you? You can forget it. I don't like you and I hope to hell to never see you again," he commanded as he stepped through the doorway.

***

Minutes later, Delmar staggered back into the courtyard.

Nona saw him entering and immediately rose and rushed over to his side. "Delmar! Thank the heavens that you are alright!"

Delmar scanned the courtyard. "This place is filled with a lot of dead people Nona, I want to find the Rose Crystal quartz and go home."

"Yes, let's go home. I already have the Rose Crystal quartz," Nona replied, with a big grin on her face.

Delmar smiled and murmured. "We've got everything?"

"Yes, we do Delmar, I believe we do."

"Nona! Delmar! Queen Calafia called as she made her way across the courtyard. She hurriedly closed the distance between them.

Anger surged up in Nona at the sound of Queen Calafia voice. The Queen hadn't been the best of hostesses. She was sure Delmar had been drugged. She defensively took a step-in front of Delmar. "What is it you want, Queen Calafia?"

"Why Nona, my friend, I come in peace," Queen Calafia said. "It appears that you were right," her tone sounded forlorn.

"About what?" Nona inquired.

"About love being, the greatest and most fiercest, power that God has ever made. Throughout time, men and women have thought the greatest gift to possess were power, treasures, kingdoms, glory and immortality."

Nona thought back to their conversation. "For thousands of years, mankind has gotten it wrong. Love is the greatest power God ever made."

Delmar nodded, as he glanced off into the distance and spoke. "What's the use of living for thousands of years without love. To do so is like living in a tomb. A tomb where you can never know love, where two people live together, share and grow old together. That is true power, true love."

"Yes, you are both wise," Queen Calafia said, as she took a few steps and looked around her surrounds. "When you were sent here, Delmar, it was for a test that you had no idea of."

Delmar looked back at her and froze. Before he could say anything, the Queen continued.

"Please let me finish. "You came here Delmar to obtain the item needed to lift a curse. You have your item, you have everything you need now to lift the curse. But what you do not know is that you have made a grave enemy."

"What?" Delmar asked taking a step forward.

"No, Delmar," Queen Calafia said, placing her hand on his shoulder. "You do not have to worry about me or my people. We are not your enemy. But you have met your enemy in this life and in your past life, be careful my friend."

Queen Calafia stared at her hands. "Nona, these hands had to remove your protective shield from Delmar. I apologize for my deceit, but it was required," she exhaled. "Delmar's enemy came to me and took something that I treasure and forced me to do her bidding. My treasure has now been returned and Delmar's enemy has been banned. I have put back your protective shield on Delmar, and my own. He will need it, for his enemy is not happy I'm afraid."

She peered up at Nona and spoke. "You and Delmar are free to leave. Siachen and Cree, are waiting for you with the horses. They will take you back to the entrance of time."

Nona and Delmar glanced at Queen Calafia.

Delmar said nothing just nodded his head and turned a walked away.

"Thank you, Queen Calafia," Nona replied, and immediately then turned and made her exit.

Chapter 23

Dawn Breaks…

The night passed, a unique dawn was being born, when the travel portal elevator landed back at Delmar's penthouse.

Nona observed Delmar as the doors opened. Delmar peered around but didn't make a move to get out of the elevator.

He appeared uneasy as he glared out at his residence, high above downtown San Jose. For some reason, he felt paralyzed.

"What is wrong Delmar?" Nona asked.

Delmar had felt a new threat, unforeseen, developing since he had his last couple of encounters with the she-devil, spirit or whatever it was. His heart was heavy with disappointment. He'd thought as soon as they obtain the last item needed the curse would instantly be lifted. "I'm disappointed and afraid," he heard himself say out loud.

Nona walked over and stood in front of him. "What are you afraid of?"

Delmar nervously blinked and finally exhaled. "I thought this would finally be over as soon as we obtained the last item. But nothing has changed. Something is after me. Something that is not of this world that…" he paused. "That feels like it wants to destroy me."

Nona felt a surge of sympathy for Delmar. He'd been through a lot. He had no idea about how things like this worked. At the end of every day, everyone needed someone to reassure them.

"Delmar, listen to me. There is still work that must be done. We must take all the items and hold the curse breaking ritual."

Nona studied his face. Delmar's eyes looked lost and unfathomable. She wished she could read his thoughts.

"Look, Delmar, tomorrow, will be the perfect night to do that. The dark moon will be high in the sky and it makes for ease in removing of curses."

"Are you sure?"

"Yes, Delmar, you see when the moon is dark this door is open making it a perfect time for ancestor worship and summoning chthonic and crossroad deities. It will be the perfect time to send back in time, whatever came out of it."

A muscle worked in Delmar's jaw. His mind was racing this whole thing was almost over. He thought about Tiara and his sons. Could they really be a family soon? "Hmmm, that sounds interesting."

After a long moment of silence, Nona spoke. "Delmar, go inside and get some rest. You'll need your strength for tomorrow night. You must be at Glenda place in San Juan Baptista tomorrow night. Before the sun sets."

"I'll get some sleep a little later," he said. "Remember, I told you, I've been curious about time travel ever since you and I started traveling using the travel portals?" He asked but didn't wait for a response, "Well, after Mistress Pleasant told me about Ye old Book Shoppe, in Berkley, I went and found the place and I got to see the guy named Pegasus. He gave me the book called "How to Never Get Lost in Time" by Herminoe Potter, in fact, I plan on bucking down and giving it a read, tonight."

"Well, that's good, but do try and get some decent rest Delmar, don't spend all your time reading," Nona said with a serious tone in her voice. "I need you rested and present at Glenda's by night fall, tomorrow."

Delmar heard the serious tone in her voice. "Okay, I'll be there. I need for this to be finished. I want my life and my family back."

Chapter 24

Tiara

Tiara Blake sat on the edge of her bed and feeling good for having gotten through her morning routine of getting her boys up, bathed, dressed and fed. She didn't even feel guilty that she had put them in hands of Odessa Johnson's granddaughter, Linda Perrin. Linda had turned out to be such a fantastic babysitter that Tiara had offered her a job as the live-in nanny.

She got up and meandered aimlessly around the house, checking the doors to make sure she'd locked them after Linda left with the boys. But the sinking sensation just wouldn't go away. A quiver shot down her body. It was her gut, it was twisting in knots again. She'd been having these strange sensations ever since she'd discovered the truth about Diademe. For some reason, Diademe kept darting up in her mind. That and that fact instinct was advising her that Delmar was in grave danger.

She turned her thoughts to Delmar, for a while now she knew her old feelings for him had never died. Was she wrong for wanting him? Then there was Diademe, why was she interested in her Delmar? Delmar was her's. He always would be.

Normally she wasn't afraid to confront difficult situations. But the thought of Diademe somehow presented a danger to her. A danger that she just couldn't put her finger on.

Her mind kept going back to the clock beside her bed. She recalled that at 3:00 a.m. she had the worst feeling in the world that Delmar needed her.

She supposed she could put off trying to see what all her feelings were about concerning Diademe, especially since she didn't know where to find her. But she knew where to find Delmar and with so much free time on her hands that was exactly what she planned to do. She was going to find Delmar and find out what was going on. She headed back to her bedroom, she needed to get dressed.

Chapter 25
A shadow crossed

Hours later, Delmar laid in bed flipping through the pages of a time travel book, he'd found in Berkley at Ye Olde Book Shoppe on Shattuck Avenue in Berkley, when a photograph fell out of the pages. He picked it up. It was an old vintage photograph of a beautiful woman. Something made him flip the photo over. It read. "Quadroons Ladies of the French Quarter in New Orleans 1805, Ava Elizabeth Tara Arceneaux."

Like a ghost brushing up against him instantaneously, he recognized the woman in the picture. How he wished he could share the picture with Tiara.

Delmar sighed heavily. The woman in the picture looked exactly like Tiara Blake. He wished Tiara was here with him so that he could show her the photo. He thought about taking the photo to show her and thought he'd best get out of bed and take a shower first.

The sun streamed through the overhead skylight in the bathroom as he brushed his teeth. He looked around admiring the bathroom it was his favorite room in the penthouse. He'd designed it himself. The length of the shower was an entire wall of glass. With an adjoining full functioning steam room, jacuzzi tub for two, his private King-sized master suite retreat, was large enough for a small family.

As his shower steamed up he turned on his music system. Soon relaxing, smooth, soft, and reassuring sounds filled the air as he stepped into the shower.

Delmar washed his face with a sudsy loofah and thought to himself about the best way to get Tiara to come over. As he rinsed his face and body with the tepid water. He thought he heard giggling. Like a woman's voice. He turned off the faucet and listened. All he heard was the quiet music playing.

"I must be imagining things," he declared under his breath and got out the shower. Grabbing his towel, he quickly dried himself and wandered over to the sink.

Delmar dried his hair and considered the mirror. Startled! He thought he caught a glimpse of a figure standing behind him. He quickly turned around and stared at the spot where the figure had been standing. It was empty.

"That's strange," he announced out loud, and spun around and finished up his daily ritual. He finished dressing and headed to the kitchen.

He stopped dead in his tracks. His front door was jarred. He remembered locking it.

"What the hell!" He yelled. "Is anybody in here?"

"Delmar it's me, Tiara! I'm in the kitchen!"

"Tiara?" Delmar said, marching into the kitchen. He looked her over from head to feet. It was the real Tiara. He was sure of it. "What are you doing here?"

"I couldn't help myself," Tiara said, making eye contact with him. "I saw your front door, standing wide-open, and thought something was wrong. So, I came in looking around. I'm so glad you are alright."

She strode over to him, carrying a huge tote bag. "Look, Delmar, there's something I need to tell you. I'm sorry…"

The relief in his voice was palpable. "No… No, don't be," Delmar assured her. "In fact, I was going to go out looking for you, shortly."

"You were?" She murmured, with a surprised look on her face.

Delmar shook his head. "Yes, I was. But first, would you like for me to help you with that tote bag? It seems heavy."

Tiara glanced at the bag she carried and knew that it was precious cargo. She didn't want it out of her sight. Besides, better to say this why she had her courage up, she thought. "I'm fine with the tote bag, it's not that heavy," she said reaching out and adjusting it.

"Suit yourself," he shrugged.

She gazed at Delmar another moment and then cleared her throat. "Look, Delmar, I came over because I was hoping to talk to you. Something strange has been happening lately."

"Excuse me?" Delmar lifted his brow. "You've experienced something? Something strange I mean?"

"Oh, yes!" She replied, shifting the tote bag hanging on her shoulder. "Maybe you could offer me a cup of coffee or something, maybe sit down and talk?"

"Yes, of course," Delmar said. "Excuse my manners, please have a seat and I'll fix us both a cup of coffee."

He went through the cabinets and cupboards until he found what he needed. Quickly he filled the electric coffee percolator with water and coffee, then closed the lid and pressed the start button.

The electric coffee percolator started making its blub-blub sound and then instantaneously the room filled with the aroma of freshly brewed coffee.

"Mmmm I love that aroma of freshly brewed coffee. The smell is so intoxicating," Tiara replied.

She rose and walked over to look at the electric coffee percolator. "Is it ready yet?"

"Hold your horses, now back to your seat young lady, I have this all under control," Delmar muttered, smiling to himself. He'd always found Tiara's naive fascination irresistible. He unplugged the percolator. He placed a gold-trimmed black china porcelain coffee pot on a tray, already loaded with cream and sugar. He grabbed two matching mugs and placed them on the tray before heading back to the table.

"There you go," he added, pouring Tiara a cup of hot coffee.

Tiara sat back down and blew on her coffee and took a sip. "Mmmm, this was worth the wait. It tastes marvelous."

Delmar took his seat and poured himself a cup of coffee before glancing back at her.

Tiara placed her mug back on the table and thought about why she came. She couldn't get the thought that Delmar had seen her leave with Zackary Vaughn out of her head. "I wasn't sure what else to do when I came over here," she finally spoke. "You see ever since I learned that you thought you saw me leaving to go home with Zackary Vaughn, that night from the club. All I can think about was how to explain to you that it wasn't me," she studied his eyes. "I mean... It looked like me. But it wasn't me. I swear!"

"I know," Delmar said shaking his head. He got up and walked over to the counter and snagged some cinnamon sticks and returned and sat back down.

Silence hung heavy between them.

Tiara blinked trying to figure out what was going on with Delmar.

Delmar cleared his throat and finally spoke. "We are under an evil curse, you and I," he eventually said.

"What?" Puzzled Tiara shook her head. "I don't understand."

He regarded her eyes. "It turns out we both had mutual ancestors who knew each other in shall we say a biblical way, just as we did in this lifetime," he hesitated. "Only our ancestors left us with a curse. Let me tell you the story as I know it from the beginning."

Slowly Delmar filled Tiara in on the story and brought her up to date. He didn't leave out anything. He even included Lady Eidothea, The White Witch of Antioch, and including his visits to the caves and Queen Calafia.

When he was done, he sat there and stared into his coffee.

"Wow, that was an amazing story," Tiara whispered. "It includes all kinds of stuff, black magic, white magic, myths, ghosts, mermaids and more. Truly incredible," her voice collapsed.

"I know it's a lot of stuff to wrap your mind around, but it's all true," he exhaled. "Until I went on this journey quest, I had no idea so much existed in this life," he hesitated and heard the voice echo in his head. *"And I had no idea how much you and my sons meant to me."*

"There is all kind of knowledge in this world, seen and unseen," Tiara said. "Don't worry Delmar, I believe you. In fact, the woman you saw leaving with Zackary Vaughn, that night, who looked exactly like me, wasn't of this world, if you know what I mean."

Delmar dragged a hand across his hair and then reached for the photo in his front pocket. "I know, I finally figure it out and I think I found a photo of your ancestor," he said placing the photo in front of her. "Flip it over and read the name."

"Quadroons Ladies of the French Quarter in New Orleans 1805, Ava Elizabeth Tiara Arceneaux."

Like a ghost brushing up against her Tiara instantly recognized he woman in the picture with her face. Standing next to her was another woman. She flipped the photo back over again.

Eva Victoria Diademe Arceneaux, *and written in very tiny letters it read. Twin daughters of James Pascal Arceneaux.*

Tiara exhaled. "They are twins! Though not identical twins but they look like sisters, it says here they are fraternal twins."

Delmar sighed heavily. "What?"

"Yes, look here, in tiny letters," Tiara pointed. "Tiara and Diademe are fraternal twin sisters."

Tiara felt her heart racing, it was like a veil was lifting as she held the ancient looking photograph. She felt like it was talking to her, telling her things. Her temple throbbed. She sensed a presence, and something brushed against her leg.

The atmosphere in the room changed drastically. It felt as if something cold, heavy and dark had been dropped on them like a heavy velvet curtain.

All at once Tiara felt herself growing sad staring back at the picture as the images flooded her thoughts. Two sisters, one man, the story was an old as time. One sister loved the man, but the man loved the other sister.

"Oh, Christ!" Tiara screamed and grabbed Delmar's arm. "Delmar what did you do?"

"What?"

She looked at him strangely. "Delmar, I see it so clearly, like a vision. You are half-naked in bed with her. I feel it. It's desire. Pure lustful desire. You are with... With Diademe!"

Delmar grabbed her hand. "I don't know what's happening, but she tried to seduce me, back in the caves, several times."

Someone began laughing. It was a woman's voice carried coldly on the air.

"There's a presence in this room," Tiara said, and thought about all the tales of the supernatural she had read in her lifetime.

"What's happening?" Delmar asked.

"I don't know Delmar but whatever you do not let go of my hand," Tiara said, gripping his hand firmly.

Instantly she remembered the tote bag containing the quilt and quickly released Delmar's hand.

"Hey, what are you doing?" Delmar asked.

"I forgot something," Tiara said reaching into the tote bag and retrieving the quilt. She shook it out over the floor.

Delmar stood up and scratched his head. "A quilt? You brought a quilt with you?"

"Keep an open mind Delmar and look closer," she said. "This just ain't no ordinary quilt. This quilt is powerful! It's straight out of the South of the Mason Dixon line and stitched by hands of a bunch of holier than thou, grandmothers from the Opelousas Quilting Guild in Opelousas Louisiana!"

"I'm supposed to get excited about a quilt with a bunch of circles on it?"

"Well, yeah, because that pattern is called the double rings or interlocking circles and it's a very old pattern of protection that dates back over thousands of years," Tiara replied. "Come sit down with me on it, Delmar."

Delmar did as he was told and slid his hand across the fabric. "So, this is a symbol of protection?"

"Yeah, and believe me Delmar, it's powerful."

A crack of thunder broke right over them, and Delmar watched as Tiara flinched. "Don't worry Tiara!" he shouted as he gripped her hand tighter.

Suddenly, a flash of red light poured in through the windows, like a red ink bomb explosion, blanketing everything around it.

The was a long silence and then a strong floral scent and cold air filled the room.

"I think our friend is here," Tiara muttered. "It must be show time," she said, reaching into her pocket, with one hand and with the other hand tightly squeezing Delmar's hand. She reached into her pocket and brought out a tiny Gris Gris bag and placed it into Delmar's shirt pocket.

"What is this? More protection?" Delmar asked, in wonder.

"Right again, and I think we're going to need all the protection we can get!" Tiara sternly said. "Don't worry it comes from a great source, in fact, it's from four sources."

"Who?" Delmar inquired.

"That would be whom," Tiara breathed out. "And they are, Glenda D'Goodwrench, Nona Laveau descendant of Marie Laveau, Consuelo Oshun of the great family of the Oshun of Santería Cuba and Catherine Marie Rousseau-La Cour of the great family of the Roussesau of Goldonna Louisiana. Who by the way, everyone knows as Grand-mere Catherine," she smiled. "Oh, yeah, by the way Grand-mere Catherine provided the quilt. The Opelousas Quilting Guild in Opelousas Louisiana is made up of a bunch of her relatives."

"Okay, I see you covered all your bases," Delmar said. "Tell me something, if you've talked to any of those ladies, you do have a sense of what we are up against, right?"

"That is correct my dear Delmar, and now your lady of this time and space is ready to do battle with my ancestor's lady of her time and space, to stop that mad heifer from taking my man," Tiara rolled her eyes. "Who would have ever thought I would have to kick a ghost woman's ass to get her to leave my man alone?"

Delmar laughed and smiled a crooked wicked sexy smile. "You would do that for me?"

"My sons do need their father," Tiara smiled softly. "And I need my man back."

Delmar leaned over and kissed her. "Tiara, please forgive me for all the stupid things I did to you and our sons. I've had a long time to think about it and I want us all to be together as a family. And yes, that means I want to marry you."

Tiara let out a sigh and hunched over her shoulders, bowing her head. She felt like she was going to cry. She waited years to hear him say those words.

Delmar tried to compose himself. *"She'd better not cry,"* he thought. It was the one thing he couldn't handle right now -- a woman's tears. "Tiara... Baby, it's gon' to be alright."

She sniffed and wiped her nose. "I've waited so long to hear you say that. Yes, I'll marry you."

A moment after she spoke a cold wind sliced the air.

"You fucked my sister!" A low shrill, quivering, penetrating dead voice filled the air and began repeating over and over. *"You fucked my sister! You fucked my sister! And it was I who wanted you!"*

Like bats out of hell, a great burst of vapor rose out of thin air and took the form of a woman with green eyes.

Tiara blinked and focused until it registered. The vapor of a woman looked familiar. A chill went through her. The woman looked like Diademe.

"Delmar," Tiara commanded. "Whatever you do don't leave this quilt, no matter what I do, you hear me?"

"You fucked my sister!" A low shrill, quivering, penetrating dead voice filled the air and began repeating over and over. *"You fucked my sister! You fucked my sister, but it was I who wanted you!"*

The specter form of Diademe, hoovered in front of Delmar in midair and in a shrill silvery voice sung out. *"My handsome man, dare we come to meet again, for to this earth I come to claim and to seek, that which is mine, by all rights I claim! For, you fowl circumcised son of Adam, man-child, on this night, you will return to me"*

Then the specter form of Diademe, started to hiss and bauble some strange language, as he eyes glowed.

She soared into the air and then returned and hoovered in front of Tiara. "So, my dear sweet sister in this life," the specter form of Diademe, hissed. "How did it feel seeing me making love to your man in your vision?"

Tiara exhaled. "I am not afraid of you, Diademe. Besides, you only projective to me your making love to Delmar, as you wanted it to be. It wasn't real, it wasn't true. Not today, nor in the days of olde. You never did sleep with Delmar or his ancestor and that is why you are here," she slowly snorted out with laughter, letting her words sink in. "I know because he told me you didn't. And in your vision to me, you looked like an unsatisfied woman, just as you do right now!"

The specter form of Diademe was pissed off as she stared back at her earth-bound sister descendant. Diademe soared into the air, coiled as if ready to strike. "Why aren't you afraid of me?" She screamed at Tiara.

Tiara took deep breaths and remained calm. She knew she was still confused and conflicted by all that had been going on. Luckily for her, Glenda, Consuelo, and Grand-mere Catherine, had all help her to understand what was happening and to show her the power within. Power that she had always possessed but never knew she did.

"Why should I fear you. Fear is the opposite of love, the sire of hatred, the gateway to darkness. You come from the darkness,

Diademe, and you need to go back, where you belong!"

The specter form of Diademe was pissed and the malicious cackle of laughter she let out sent a child through Tiara.

Out the corner of her eye Tiara, Tiara saw a vision one that was part real world, like an illusion flashing through her mind. She saw them making love, Delmar's naked body with scratches on his back from a woman's fingernails. His mouth swollen from kissing. Rage shot through her like octane in her veins as she saw the two of them together. It was Diademe fucking Delmar.

A chill went through Tiara she understood now how Diademe came to do battle. She was going to fuck with her head. She intended to use her supernatural evil to attack the mind and the body.

Quickly Tiara shook out her thoughts and glance over at Delmar, he hadn't a clue of what just happened. The *gris-gris* bag Grand-mere Catherine had given her was working. Delmar was in a trance.

Diademe specter form let out a snort of laughter. "Listen to me Tiara, Delmar isn't right for you. He needs to go back with me."

Tiara turned to look at Diademe, two could play at the game she was playing. Slowly she closed her eyes and shut out her hearing to the outside world. Though she shut down her hearing she could hear and sense everything around her.

Slowly she started making the rhythmic sound over and over inside her head, upon her consciousness. Her instincts started to fire making her connection with her inner self stronger. As she prepared herself to fight in the battle. The next thing she realized she was standing in the physical plane, free of time and space. Dressed in jeans and a sweat shirt surrounded by light, ready for battle.

The next thing she knew she was closed in on all sides by darkness and she saw the man and woman. It was as if she was watching like a spectator. It was her and Delmar, they were naked, making love. Instantly she understood why she'd brought their lovemaking scene into existence. She needed for Diademe to see what real true love making was.

"Stop it! You're fucking him!" Diademe specter form spat out a bone chilling scream.

With an explosive lunge she raged over to Tiara was fiercely determined to sear her body with all her rage.

Tiara eluded her and stepped out the way. "You can't have my mind, body, soul or my man's," she commanded. "Look at how me and Delmar are together. It's something you will never have."

As if on cue, Tiara's vision of her and Delmar making love became vivid and real as Delmar began licking and kissing down her neck humming and moaning softly as he stroked her soft flesh, before his lips clasped around a nipple and sucked hard before he pulled her down over his naked heated body, thrust hard and plunged deep into her.

"Stop it! Stop it! You whore of Jezebel!" The specter form of Diademe went horror movie crazy screaming and howling her discontent.

Tiara had no time to enjoy the feeling of being triumphant because the next thing she knew everything went haywire when she felt herself being thrown violently through the air. Her arms and legs flying through space. The last thing she remembered was her own voice screaming in pain, when she hit the ground.

Chapter 26

Breaking the Curse...

That same night, back in the old town of San Juan Bautista, Glenda D'Goodwrench husband Scott Irishman-Jackson, finished lighting the torches and stroked the back of Pinky the cat, as he watched as his wife Glenda, Nona, Consuelo, and Grand-mere Catherine, took their work seriously, as he peeked into the dark cave, in their backyard, that his wife Glenda referred to as her office.

The cave glowed with the light of hundreds of torches. With its smooth stone circular floor and standing stone walls, it resembled a small prehistoric Stonehenge monument from Wiltshire, England.

"My love," Irishman-Jackson declared. "Would you care for me to bring you, ladies, anything else?"

"Thank you, my love, but I've bothered you enough, we have all that we need."

"Fine, then I will leave you to your task, should you need me, you've only had to call," Irishman-Jackson said, as Pinky the cat purred softly, and jumped to the floor from his hands. He grinned smugly knowing Pinky would stay back to watch over his wife and her friends. If he was needed, Pinky would come and fetch him immediately. He turned and made his exit.

Nona glanced up watching Irishman-Jackson making his exit and walked over to the heavy wooden door and grabbed the handle. Something propelled her to take a look at the full moon making its way across the sky. She recalled what she'd learned about the moon being a gateway to traveling using a transporting portal, opening the gates to other realms. She hastily closed and fastened the door and walked back to the table.

Earlier she'd placed the last of the items she collected with Delmar on the table. Now it was time to add them to the smoldering black cauldron. Quickly she reached for the first item. It was Lady Eidothea fish scale. She added it to the bubbling black cauldron. Next, she added the healing love herb they'd gotten from the White Witch of Antioch. And finally, she slowly poured Queen Calafia, Crystal Rose Quartz stones into the bubbling black cauldron.

"Do you think this will work?" Nona asked as she watched Glenda carefully stir and chatted the curse breaking mantra.

Glenda smiled. "You can break the curse with these items, yes," she paused. "But at some point, the spell will dissipate entirely, because nothing manmade can stand up to the power of the infinite Divine."

Mist spread at the base of the cauldron, as the four ladies stood in front of it. Glenda, Nona, Consuelo, and Grand-mere Catherine's eyes were held spellbound as power shimmered brighter and higher over the bubbling huge black pot.

Glenda watched anxiously as the kettle bubbled as steamed escaped and dissipated into the air.

Suddenly a vision of lighting flashing high above bubbling black cauldron caught her attention. "Oh, my goodness ladies, come and look at this! I'm afraid we may have forgotten something!"

"What is it?" Consuelo asked.

"Look at the vision," Glenda replied. "It's Tiara and Diademe."

"Yes, I see," Consuelo replied. "Looks like they are about to fight!"

"That's just it," Glenda said. "I forgot to train her to fight. We've got to work quickly to break the curse."

"But it looks to me like Tiara's doing alright," Nona cried. "And she is already in the throes of battle. If you didn't teach her how to fight against darkness, who did?"

"I did!" Grand-mere Catherine quickly answered. "But Glenda is right, we need to work quickly to break the curse. Because I'm not sure if Tiara is able to handle a fight for the long haul," she shrugged, as her thoughts preyed upon her. She heard her mind say. "Tiara has not been trained to fight with demons and other sorts."

Consuelo studied Grand-mere Catherine in silence for a moment, she could see the concern on her face. She took a deep breath and leaned over and touched Grand-mere Catherine's shoulder. "My friend," she gently said. "You are concerned that Tiara won't just be fighting with her dead sister, Diademe, right?"

Grand-mere Catherine gasped. "You know as well as I do that if Diademe, came over from the other side, she may not have come alone. Diademe is not the problem, it's what she might have brought with her, who will be the real problem."

Consuelo frowned "You are right when Delmar's ancestor came through we were concerned and then Common visited Glenda later and confirmed it. Something did come through. But we still don't know what or who it is."

"That's the reason I'm afraid. You see I gave Tiara instructions for fighting Diademe, but what if another demon came through or a fallen angel? I didn't give her instructions on how to handle them."

"Relax, Consuelo assured her. "We should have the curse broken by then."

"I sure hope so," Grand-mere Catherine shouted. "Still I think we should tell Glenda and Nona, that Tiara has only had the basic training on how to fight dead people."

Consuelo nodded agreement. "Come let us go and tell them."

Chapter 27

The Magic of Love...

Transfixed by magic and power, the specter from of Diademe let loose her explosive anger flinging dust and debris in the wake of her temper tantrum, as she flings Tiara into the air.

"You whore of Jezebel!" She yelled like a crazed horror movie starlet about to perform the greatest scene of her life.

"Do you have to call me names," Tiara asked, moaning as she pushed herself off the ground. "Can't we just get along and you take your ain't got no man dead ass, back home?"

"Shut Thee up heifer!" Diademe screeched out.

Tiara grinned. "That would be heifer who's got a man to you, you no man heifer!"

Tiara spread her arms and drew in power. She was thankful for the training Grand-mere Catherine had given her. She sent forth a thought form of the power she needed. She chanted and prayed as she had been instructed to do and felt the power. She harassed it and watched as the forces of energy began to spin faster and faster. She felt the oscillation of the power. It was strong and powerful.

She felt it's energy and raised her arms high above her shoulders and sent the brilliant light hurling at Diademe. She didn't wait to see if the power she released him its target when she turned and ran looking for a haven to hide.

The radiant light of power soared through the air flying with such speed and vibration space and found its target.

"Ahhhh cramp….! Ouch! That hurt!"

Tiara herd Diademe yelling before she heard the loud thug sounding as Diademe hit the ground.

The smell of dust and Sulphur carried on the air. Tiara looked out from her hiding place and saw shimmering light showering down all around them.

"Nice trick," Diademe muttered.

"Thanks," Tiara said, surprised by her efforts.

Diademe got up off the ground. "Where did you learn how to harness power like that?"

Tiara just saluted. "I don't really know. I guess it's beginners luck."

Diademe paced in front of her a short distance away. She thought maybe it was better to have a truce with her earth-bound ancestor. "I saw the way you and Delmar are together," her voice was a solemn whisper. "The way the two of you look at each other and hold each other. You've got it," she hesitated. "Love, I mean."

What Tiara understood at moment was what living people whined so much about. The power of love. The desire for love coming from Diademe was so great, she could feel how it made her miserable. She was miserable because she had no one to love. Tiara didn't know what to say or to do. She said a small prayer for strength in knowing.

Tiara had never given much thought to ghost or if they had feelings. But watching Diademe she could tell the quality of light around her was changing, fading even.

Diademe finally spoke. "Now, you can see why I want to fuck him," she hesitated and said slowly, as tears started streaming down her face. "I mean make love to Delmar. You have that rare chemistry, love, and magic that's been perfected through space and time. I want to feel it. I want to feel that love. It's powerful…"

"Yes, it has the power to defeat darkness," Tiara injected. "And I can see just as you crave it, you fear it."

"I know," Diademe said with understanding. "I have tried to come to this earth plane many, many times for hundreds of years to try and experience the powerful feeling of love. But he…"

Tiara stared back at Diademe and noticed the blank stare of fear on her face. "He?" She curiously asked. "Who is he?"

In a swirl of smoke, blue binding light coalesced alone with the smell of Sulphur and formed taking shape until a handsome solid looking human man appeared before her.

His dark brown hair had golden highlights was flowing over his bronze shoulders. His face held beautiful chiseled features, like an angel's face. He wore the robes in the color of blood and power over his over six-foot-three-inches tall, muscular toned lean frame.

For a moment, Tiara was too overwhelmed to move, she'd never seen a man so beautiful before.

"Tiara, my ancestor sister," Diademe said, lightly through a pulse shudder. "Meet Osmodeus, the angel of lust. Some in the Bible referred to him as Asmodai, the false god for whom the Syrian Hamathites made an idol too."

Osmodesu laughed. "And do not forget Diademe, some say that I am a cambion, the offspring of the union between Agrat Bat Mahlat, a succubus, and King David."

Tiara looked at him. He radiated raw sexual energy like nothing she'd ever seen before. Wishful thinking got the best of her and she exclaimed. "So, Osmodesu, you've come to take Diademe back to her home?"

A crack of wicked laughter like she'd never heard came out of Osmodesu's mouth.

"You are too funny!" Osmodesu snickered out a chuckle.

"Yes, she is Osmodes, and this one is quite obtuse," Diademe replied.

Diademe turned her attention to Tiara and took a deep breath. "For, you see sister. It was I who went to Eve Laveau and got the spell that became the curse on the house of Deveraux."

"What? And who is Eve Laveau?" Tiara inquired, shaking her head.

Diademe laughed fiercely. "She was a distant relative of the great Marie Laveau and she knew her Hoodoo well. She gave me the curse that I used on the house of Deveraux when Delmar's ancestor betrayed me! By not marrying me!"

"What are you talking about?" Tiara asked, but didn't wait for a response. "Delmar's ancestor was supposed to marry me in his former life."

A burst of wicked laughter blurted loudly from Diademe. "You! You! You! It was never about you! It was always about me! You stupid heifer!" She wailed. "And now I'm going to have what should have been mine, long ago."

For a moment, Tiara thought she had heard her wrong and then she turned and looked at the spot where she last saw Diademe and she was gone.

"Ah, what the fuck!" Tiara yelled annoyed. "Where did she go?"

Osmodesu snickered out a chuckle. "She just seemed to have flown away. And by the way, I'm here to keep you busy, while

Diademe has her way with your man."

At the meaning of what Osmodesu had spoken. Tiara turned her attention.

When she glanced off into the distance and she saw Diademe snaking around Delmar, as he sat on the quilt. She watched as Diademe finally stood in front of him and stripped naked. When she realized he wasn't responding she dropped to her knees and begin a battle with him trying to unzip his pants.

"Yes, my dear looks like Diademe is getting down to business," Osmodeus gave off a malicious laugh. "And I'm am the man for you to have a good fuck with. Right here and right now. You see it's exactly why I came."

Osmodeus hurried and closed the distance between them, howling the whole time, while doing it.

With an immediate panic, Tiara turned and tried to find her safe haven. She ran as fast as she could. She felt Osmodesu's hot breath inches from her, as she ran.

Snapping into action she braced herself and took off running in circles. A hideous waltz was taking place as she and Osmodeus circled around and around.

All at once everything went into slow motion as she felt his energy burst into motion so fast it seem like he jumped like a jackrabbit flying through the air before tackling her.

Tiara offered a quick prayer before she let loose her mind like a movie playing a series of vision, just before she hit the ground. A sinister slide show was playing in her head.

The impact of hitting the ground was so great, Tiara thought she had shattered every bone in her body as she laid there. Then she felt Osmodeus collapsing on top of her.

Two bodies lying on top of one another. Like two people who had to hold on to each other. She felt the weight of Osmodesu. She could smell his intoxicating scent.

"Open those pretty eyes of yours beautiful and look at me," Osmodeus demanded. "I've got to get you naked," he moaned, as she struggled, he kissed the exposed column of her throat. "Mmmmm, you taste yummy!"

Tiara struggled and Osmodeus hand reached up and grabbed her by her hair and forced her to look at him.

He licked his lips as he focused on her. He grabbed her hand and pressed it on his erection. "Oh, yeah,

we gonna fuck! Sweetness. By the way, I ain't into condoms," he growled, as he hooked his hands into her jeans with his thumbs and began pulling them off.

"Tiara! Tiara! Wake up, Tiara! Danger! Danger!" A familiar woman's voice softly called. "Remember your training! Remember your training. You know what to do!"

All at once Tiara's brain came back online. She squeezed her eyes shut and pushed her body to the side and forced the vision clearer in her mind.

"Glenda! Nona! Consuela! Grand-mere Catherine, is that you?" Tiara moaned. "Is this a dream?"

"Hush child, get up. The fight is not over." She heard their voices in Unisom. *"But you have the power! You can defeat him! Banish him from your mind! Use your words!"*

All at once, Tiara became acutely aware of Osmodesu' body and his masculine scent. It brought out something in her. She rolled over and faced him and brought her had to his face. She pressed the palm of her hand in his face and yelled.

"There is nothing my love will not do! For my love who waits for me is true! I take my gifts, my talents, my love to heart! For me and my love, we shall not part! Unlike you, Osmodeus, I know to whom I am faithful too! Whom I am true! Faithful, mind, body and soul! Faithful, mind, body and soul!" She repeated like a mantra. "And I will have what I hold true! What I want most in life! I will, and I take back my life! I will! I will, so smote thee be! "

"As I will," Osmodesu declared. "Just as soon as I fuck you!"

"No! As you will not, for my oath is to me, to those that I love and who love me! So, smote it be! Be gone with thee Osmodesu, back to hell I send thee, as it is, so it shall be! So, I will thee back to hell! I command thee!" She fiercely declared, pressing her palm into his face.

"Holy shit! What the fuck did you do to me?" Osmodesu raged.

His voice became short and shallow. As terror struck deep inside him like a vampire who's been hit with a wooden stake laced with a poisonous venom. "What's happening!"

Fast, everything was going so fast like a dream, Osmodesu body grew limp, light, he looked like he was struggling to focus. His eyes stayed transfixed on her.

As her mind threatened to propel her into immobility. She heard her self-declare through delirium. "I transfixed you with the power of love! Now go back to hell, I command thee!"

After several minutes she heard herself say. *"Pull it together, Tiara! Pull it together,"* as said to herself, as she rolled onto her back and blinked trying to focus her vision.

Osmodesu was gone. She tilted her head and looked into the distance of where she last saw Diademe. She was gone too.

All at once she remembered where she was and why. She sat up and realized she wasn't hurt. *"This is unreal,"* she thought, *"I don't have a scratch on me."*

All at once her brain remembered what she had been doing and her body responded. She rose up and glanced around. She saw Delmar in the distance still lying on the quilt. She headed over towards him.

"Delmar!" Tiara shouted as she drew closer. She yelled his name again and still, he did not answer.

Reaching him she dropped down on the quilt and shook him. "Delmar! Delmar! Can you hear me?"

And still, he did not answer. Tiara felt her heart stop. The air around her felt dry and thick. She felt the fear deep in her gut. Had breaking the curse somehow backfired?

"Oh, my God! What is wrong with you Delmar? Why can't you hear me? I don't know what to do!"

In anguish, she heard her voice echoing around her. She closed her eyes and drew in a long deep breath, and let it out slowly calming her mind. She focused and centered her mind and felt the rhythm of her heartbeat. She concentrated and then she heard the beat of Delmar's heart. It was faint.

Tiara, then she felt a warm breath at her ear and it whispered. "Kiss him, my child. Just as the prince kissed sleeping beauty. Wake Delmar from the spell."

Tiara's jaw dropped open before she caught herself. She glanced around self-consciously trying to see who had whispered in her ear. She wasn't sure what to do.

She glanced up at Delmar and the took one of his hands and pressed it to her breast and then closed her eyes and leaned into him. "Oh, my love," she softly whispered. "May you please remember me with this kiss," she said as she pressed her lips to his.

At first, nothing happened and then slowly Delmar responded, kissing, licking and nibbling on her lips.

Humming softly, Delmar teased her. "Interesting, very interesting. Either your lips taste like fried chicken, or I'm one hell of a hungry man, right now."

Tiara laughed and kissed him hard.

Delmar blew out a long breath, "No offense, but the last thing I remember was you were telling me not to leave this quilt. It feels like I've been here for days." He grunted in annoyance. When are you going to take me home and feed me, woman?"

"Come on, Delmar, let's go home," Tiara commanded, getting up off of the quilt. She knew intuitively that the curse had been broken. It was time for them to go home.

Epilogue
Black and White Masquerade Ball

Tiara smiled with delight at the view of the Transamerica Pyramid building. It was still all decked out in white lights for the Christmas Holiday. They were just finishing up dining at the Embarcadero building's famous Solar Eclipse restaurant located at the top of the building, before heading downstairs to the Black and White Masquerade Ball.

The Black and White Masquerade Ball was held each year on December 31, and held a stunning display of acts, costumes, fantasy exhibits, with a vast array of storytellers, musical performances, hypnotizing dancers and much more.

Just then Camille and Eris walked over.

"I have so much to tell you guys," Tiara blurted, hugging her two best friends. Camille and Eris, as they walked down the staircase.

"Do you think Delmar invited enough people?" Camille asked.

"My sentiments exactly," Eris agreed. "We were seated way down at the far end of the table. There had to be fifty people between us, and I couldn't get a word in edgewise."

"Is that so, Eris?" Camille asked, but didn't wait for a response. "As I recall you kept a regular amount of communication with a woman named, queen what's her name."

"Oh, she replied her name was, Queen Calafia Jackson. She added something about being a distant relative of Glenda D'Goodwrench Jackson's husband, Scott Irishman-Jackson. But the woman had some of the coldest hands I ever touched."

"That's where you went wrong, touching her hands," Camille said. "By the way Tiara, what's up with that Lady Eidothea character? Some guys were treating her like royalty?"

Tiara frowned trying to catch the familiar faces her best friends were chatting about. She knew who the people they were talking about really were, but felt she should not tell her two best friends the truth until well after the New Year's Celebration was over.

"Yeah, Tiara," Eris added. "What's up with Delmar escorting Lady Eidothea, all evening? Doesn't she realize he's your man?"

Before Tiara had time to respond back someone touched her shoulder. She stopped abruptly and turned and looked up.

"You're Tiara Blake?" A man with deep green eyes asked.

"Yes," Tiara nodded. "Who are you?"

"Let me introduce myself. I'm Dr. Sydney Titor, your fiancé, Delmar Devereau was to escort my date Lady Eidothea here tonight and I can't seem to find them."

Eris' mouth dropped opened. "I've heard of you. You're the Dr. Sydney Titor, the famous paranormal investigator. The one who's regularly on that TV program, Bay Area Investigates the Paranormal!"

"You are perfectly correct, my dear," Dr. Titor said. "And you are?"

"I'm Eris Simeon, Tiara's best friend."

"Now wait a minute Eris, you forgot I'm standing here and I'm just as much Tiara's best friend as you are," Camille added. "By the way Dr. Titor, I'm Camille Baptiste-Garcia."

"Nice to meet both of you, Eris and Camille. Now if I can get back on track, I believe I was asking Tiara if she could help me find my date?"

Tiara laughed. "You bet I can Dr. Titor, your date, Lady Eidothea and my fiancé Delmar should be downstairs in the main ballroom waiting for you."

"Thank you, my dear, Tiara," Dr. Titor, said taking her hand and kissing it. "Now if you ladies will excuse me, I'm off to find my date."

He turned and regally glided down the staircase giving off an electrifying quintessential air of sophistication found only by leading men in the movies.

Eris sighed heavily. "Damn that man reminds me of some quintessential leading man in a movie. I wish I could take him home with me and bang the hell out of him all night!"

Tiara stiffened. "Eris Simeon, I've never heard you talk so brazen before. It is completely out of character."

"Yeah," Eris exhaled. "You're right. Life is funny. You

know it's seems so weird here you'r engaged and acting like a settled woman. And Camille's married and acting like a married woman. And me, well looks like now that the two of you are off the market. I'm acting like the sex crazed femme fatale."

The three friends broke out laughing.

Finally, Eris spoke. "Still I can't understand you didn't feel the least bit jealous that Lady Eidothea was all up on your man like that, Tiara?"

"Eris," Tiara said shaking her head. "Like I told you early it's no big deal. Delmar promised to escort Lady Eidothea, until her date arrives. Besides, am I not the woman walking around with a four carat flawless and colorless, VS1 diamond ring." She added, holding up her engagement ring.

Tiara was on the verge of further arguing her point when Delmar walked over smiling and offering her his hand.

"Well my love my duty to Lady Eidothea is done. Her date has arrived and you won't believe who the gentleman is?"

"Dr. Sydney Titor, the famous paranormal investigator, " The three friends replied, laughing in unisom.

"How did you ladies know?" Delmar laughed.

"Dr. Titor, came over and introduced himself," Tiara said, taking Delmar's arm.

All at once a waiter walked over to them with a tray of drinks. "Would any of you care for a pineapple martini?" The waiter asked.

"I would love a glass," Tiara said, picking up a glasss and taking a long relieve sip. At the strain of feeling like everyone was staring, she looked up.

Tiara was on the verge of asking what was up, when she felt Delmar's hand tightly squeeze around hers. She looked into his eyes.

"Marry me, Tiara," Delmar said.

Totally confused Tiara looked back into his eyes. "But I already said I would," she held up her ring finger and pointed to her four carat engagement ring. "See!"

"I mean right here, right now. In front of all of our friends and family."

With trembling fingers, Tiara looked around into the swarms

of people around her and realized that they were family and friends and they knew what was happening.

Tiara smiled warmly at the friends and family surrounding her and felt tears of joy brimming behind her eyelids. They were all there to be apart of her happiness.

"Yes! Yes! Delmar, I'll marry you right here and now!" Tiara stated.

Delmar pulled her close and yelled. "Where's that minister?"

At the sound of Delmar's commanding voice, a minister stepped in front of the happy couple and said. "Dearly beloved, we are gather here today, in the sight of God, and in the face of this company to join together, this man, Delmar Devereaux and this woman, Tiara Blake in Holy matriomony…"

It was a hard thing to watch, from the back of the room. The brooding man with the large build and dark eyes thought as he looked upon the festivities. His dark eyes stayed fixed on the couple getting married. He was too stubborn to just let things go. Besides, he never did believe in happy ever after. It was just a matter of time before one of them messed things up and he would be right there when they did to have what he wanted.

"Good Lord! What are you doing here? I can't believe you were invited?"

"Hello to you too, Desmond Garcia. I understand I should congratulate you on marrying Camille. So, sorry I missed your wedding."

"Well, Brandon Stone, I don't recall Camille ever sending you an invitation," Desmond stated. "No hard feelings, I hope?"

"Of course not," Brandon said.

"So, what brings you here tonight? Got an invitation to this wedding?"

Brandon worked his jaw trying to think of something to say. "Well... I huh! No I didn't get an invitation, Desmond. I was just downstairs at the Black and White Masquerade Ball, in the main ballroom and remembered how beautiful the view was of San Francisco from the top of the Embarcdero Building at night. So, I just thought I'd have a look."

Desmond nodded and took a deep breath. "I'm trying to be delicate here. I'm afraid I was put in charge of security, by Delmar and I take my duties seriously."

"No, worries, that's understandable. It was about time for me to head back downstairs to the main ballroom anyway," Brandon said, dryly. "See you a round, Desmond."

"Likewise," Desmond replied, watching Brandon Stone make his exit. He watched and made sure Brandon got on the elevator. When the door closed, Desmond breathed out a sigh of relief. Thankful that things didn't turn ugly.

As the elevator door closed in front of him, Brandon Stone, he felt his heart lurched in his chest. He tilted his head in regret and closed his eyes, thinking about the moment he watched the woman he loved marry another man. *It wouldn't be for long. He was going to make sure of that,* he thought, as his hands balled up beside him in fists of rage. Feeling the rage building up inside him, he knew no angel born in heaven could break the rage that he was building deep inside him.

"Tiara is mine!" Brandon screamed out in the empty elevator. "I'll make you pay for stealing what belongs to me, Delmar Devereaux," he muttered under his breath.

The End

About **the Author J.A. JACKSON**

J.A. JACKSON is an author who lives in an enchanted little house she calls home in the Northern California foothills. She fell in love with writing as a small child. She was born in Arkansas, raised in Chicago, Illinois and comes from a family rich in story tellers. She spent over ten years working in the non-profit sector where she wrote grants, press releases and contributed many stories to their newsletter. She was their Newsletter editor for over ten years. She loves growing roses, a good pot of hot tea, chocolate, magical stories, suspense stories, ghost stories, and reading Jane Austen again and again in her past time. Please write her at P.O. Box 62323 Sunnyvale, CA 94088.

PSEUDONYM: J. A. Jackson

Email Address: jerreecejackson@gmail.com
jerreecejackson@yahoo.com

Dear *Gentle Readers*

Dear Gentle Readers, Fans, Family and Friends,

Reviews for my books are what this author needs… Let me explain.

In an effort to provide you with the most honest information about me. I confess I am a self-published author.

That's right, I am committed to writing a story, a novel every chance I get (hopefully I will put out two to three books a year). Even though I have a whacked-out, frenetic, hectic schedule as do many others. I persevere. I am committed to writing my stories.

With that said, I'd like to make a request of you my gentle readers, followers, friends, and family. I appreciate that you read my books. And I need you to please go to Amazon.com or KINDLE and review my book.

I appreciate that you read my books. And I need you to please go to and review my book.

I will be truthful if you do. I would like for you to help me.

Your kindness to me in reviewing my books would go a long way in helping me continue my self-publishing journey.

Thank you for all that you do. I truly appreciate you!

Sincerely,

J. A. Jackson

Email: jerreecejackson@gmail.com

Books **by J. A. Jackson**

A Geek an Angel Series

The Deceiver

The Proposition

The Grand Hotel

Lovers, Players, & The Seducer

Lovers, Players, Revenge (Book II)

The Mistress of Desire
& The Orchid Lover Book I
The Deceiver's Secret

When A Taker *Dreams*

Diamond at Midnight (Release 2018)

Thank you for all that you do. I truly appreciate you!

www.ingramcontent.com/pod-product-compliance
Lightning Source LLC
Chambersburg PA
CBHW032012170626